THE
DJ CHRONICLES
A Life Remixed

Aaron Traylor
"DJ O2-N"

PORT HOLE PUBLICATIONS
Polson, Montana

Cover Design by Adam Langer

Music lyrics gratefully acknowledged;
Some have been altered to fit story:

"Gonna Make You Sweat," C&C Music Factory
"Jesus Loves Me," Public Domain
"Give It Away," Red Hot Chili Peppers
"Dancing in the Street," Van Halen/David Lee Roth
"Runnin' With the Devil," Van Halen/David Lee Roth

DEDICATED TO

MOLLY
The one who distracted me from all of this,
if only for a brief while,
to teach me what love and responsibility are all about.
I thank you the most.

AND TO

HERBERT GUNDERSON
My Grandfather
This book would never have been possible
were it not for the stories of God's awesome love
that you shared with me.
I miss you, I love you and I thank you.

A NOTE FROM THE AUTHOR

Though some of the names, places and events have been altered or combined, this story is based on my own insider observations and experiences in the radio industry and the underground music scene of my generation.
It is my hope that what I have learned through my personal journey will benefit all who love music and seek the ultimate meaning of life.

PROLOGUE

We couldn't stay in one place for too long. We had to keep moving or Security would be all over us.

Eddie and I had once again crossed enemy lines. This time we flew in below the radar, low enough to buy us some time so we could distribute our product.

We had to wear sunglasses or our condition would tip off anyone who looked into our eyes. It was all over our faces: the rush had kicked in just moments ago.

Upon elusively entering through the mall employee entrance, the least monitored hallway of the Northtown Shopping Center, I had instructed Eddie to infiltrate deeper into the shoppers' corridors and to be efficient, yet selective, while I drifted behind near the exit doors. If I were to enter any further I'd be done for.

Fortunately Eddie hadn't been identified as an accomplice yet.

Before we executed this dangerous task I had to remind him that not just anyone could receive our supply, only those who fit the profile. They had to look the part: young, hip, and without parental accompaniment. If a father or mother were to see what we were distributing, our enterprise would be pulled out from underneath us.

"Dookie!"

Uh oh. Busted. My cover was blown. I pushed my sunglasses higher on my nose, lowered my ball cap, and pretended to ignore the girls yelling at me from behind the Pretzel Time counter, convinced I could run and never get caught. My synthetic high made me capable of outrunning anything, I thought.

Invincible. I was invincible!

"Dookie!"

There was no way to avoid the greetings. I had to sneak past the sea of back-to-school shoppers to greet my repeat customers and to curb any more shouting of my name. Sneaking, however, is not my specialty. When you are nearly seven feet tall, it's difficult to blend. Eddie was better at being incognito. With his thick, nappy afro tucked under his hat, he had already made it to the other end of

the mall without getting caught and had distributed nearly half of
what we came in with.

I paged Eddie on his two-way radio: *"ttffz...*the mission has
been compromised! I repeat! Mission compromised! Fall back! Fall
back...*fftzz"*

Though he was half-a-block away, I could see him push the
earpiece deeper into his ear. He raised his hands in the air,
indicating that he could barely catch what I just said. He was out of
range.

It was then that I saw two security guards round the corner
and head in my direction. I quickly wheeled around and knelt down
to tie my already tied shoe. The two guards stopped right behind
me. I could hear them talking about some interference on their
walkie-talkies. I could have sworn that Eddie and I had
programmed our two-ways on a different channel than theirs, but
maybe we hadn't.

*"thfftz...*Dookie...come in. Come in, Dookie...*ffttz"*

I froze in position and cupped my earpiece to keep the sound
muffled. That didn't help since his voice blasted from the guards'
walkie-talkies.

"Dookie! Come here." The two girls behind the counter waved
at me.

Using facial gestures to signal my distress I stayed crouched
while the frenzied last minute school shoppers nearly bumped me
over. The girls soon noticed the security guards, who stood just
five feet away from me on the other side of the hall, fiddling with
their antennas. As I returned my two-way to my belt, my eyes
pleaded with the girls for their assistance. They soon acknowledged
my suffering and came to my rescue.

"SHOPLIFTER!" one of them screamed, pointing toward the
Foot Locker down the corridor. The rent-a-cops quickly jumped
into action and darted down the hallway.

"You know you are crazy, right?" the blond pretzel purveyor
said with a smirk. "You really shouldn't be here. If you get caught
you are *so* up the creek."

2

"So, since we got the narks off your back, you should hook us up with a freebie!" added the young brunette after she handed change and cheese dip to a hungry customer.

"Are you kidding? If I passed out freebies to everyone I know, we'd be out of business. Twenty bucks, take it or leave it."

"Twenty bucks?" the blonde squealed. "That's outrageous!"

"Supply and demand, baby. Supply and demand," I said.

"Yeah, but what if it's no good?" she objected. "The last one, man, there was just no energy to it. You know?"

"Maybe, but you see, it's better when you do it with a whole bunch of your friends."

"All right, then half off. C'mon, give us the homey hook up. You know we deserve it," she argued, while she adjusted her floppy pretzeler hat.

"Whatever," I said, rolling my eyes. "It's not happening."

The brunette leaned over the counter and looked down the hall at the Foot Locker. "Well, we could easily make your supply a little more difficult to demand."

"Oh, so it's like that, huh?" I asked sarcastically.

"Yeah, it's like that. SHOPLIFTER!" she bellowed before I was able to clamp my hand over her mouth.

"Very funny," I groaned. "All right. All right. Half off. Take it or leave it."

"Me, too?" asked the blonde.

"Are you crazy?" I yelled.

"SECUR…"

"Fine! Fine! Half! That's it! That's all!"

All of a sudden the girls' eyes got huge. They returned to their work and pretended to ignore me.

"*ttffzz*…Mission accom..accomplished…Dookie, wus yer location? I'm next to the exit…exit. Chillin' by the exit…where are you? *fftzz*…"

I reached again for my two-way only to feel it being pulled from my belt by someone else.

"Ah, finally. I've been waiting entirely too long for this

moment to arrive," said a familiar voice.

I choked as I realized that none other than Sergeant Conrad of the Spokane Police stood behind me. With a nervous grin, I turned to face him.

"Conrad, how are you?" I said. "Just doing a little school shopping before I hit the books, you know. Reading, Writing, 'Rithmetic?" I pulled a pen off the counter and stuck it in his pocket protector.

"Uh-huh. I'm sure you are hoping the teacher will grade on a curve," he replied. "Not exactly keeping the highest grade point average lately, are we? In fact," he said as he placed the pen back on the counter without losing eye contact, "I hear you gave up the college life for these wild parties you're so hot on."

"Yo, TJ Hooker, best be...best be backin' off my homey, right?" yelled Eddie, who was now jumping up and down like a pogo stick behind Conrad. "Don't you gotta go write sp...sp...sp..speeding tickets to the mall walkers? Let us do our biz and we will be outtah yo hair, you Robo Cop wanna-be, Clint Eastwood imitatin', Warren G regulatin' po-po who ain't got nuttin' better to do, nuttin' better to do than to roll up on my boy actin' like Barney Fife with a v...v...vengeance."

I cringed as fire snapped through Conrad's eyes. Eddie was out of control, and I would surely pay for it.

"Empty your back pack!" demanded Conrad, grabbing Eddie by the collar.

"What? Why? I didn't steal nothing," Eddie defended, twisting helplessly in the big man's grip. "I know my rights. Ferg...for...forget you, sucka!"

Conrad ripped the bag away from Eddie's shoulder.

"Ah, man. What's the dilly? Can't a brother get some rights? Rodney King! Rodney King!"

"Shut up!" Conrad barked. "Let's see what you're carrying *this* time."

He unzipped the bag and dropped the contents on the floor. The bundles were wrapped in sealed plastic shipping bags in stacks of two-hundred-and-fifty and five-hundred. He knelt down to examine the product, "Holy...man, you're going all out this time. How much does this stuff cost anyway?"

"It doesn't matter. You aren't going to throw 'em away, are you?" I pleaded. "I had to have this stuff shipped...really expensive!"

"Man, when we threw a party in *my* day we didn't need stuff like this," Conrad said. "We did it the old fashioned way. We just called our friends and invited them over. Nowadays no one will even consider going to a party without one of these to entice them. You have to spend all this money on these UV protected, glossy paper, full color flyers with all these crazy psychedelic designs, crazy fonts, and an enormous roster of performers. *DJ Halo's Record Release Party*," he read. "Hmmm...whatever happened to the good ol' monster mash.?"

Eddie was seething. "See? This is why my boy is s...s...s...still on top. He goes the extra mile to get the w...word out about his parties. He don't skimp on the fine details. Everything he does is larger than life, dog, and he don't need no radio station to back up his reputation no mo'."

"Yeah, and if it weren't for Dookie all we'd have are keggers and how *boring* is that?" the blonde added, while tying raw pretzels into perfect knots. "He has done wonders for our scene."

"Can we go now?" I asked as I gingerly pulled the flyers away from the apprehensive sergeant and turned for the exit.

"Fine!" he growled. "Take your propaganda and your sorry selves out of here! If I catch you again, I'll haul you in!"

I clomped away, scarcely believing my luck. But then he called out, "Hey Big Man, Aaron! Oh yeah...I mean *Dookie*! You've changed, haven't you? You're becoming more like DJ Halo every day."

I winced, but raised my chin, as though his comment didn't sting.

His voice grew dimmer as Eddie and I hurried away. But I could not fail to hear the righteous observation that trailed me down the hall: "I thought I knew you. Now all I see is another lost soul. Maybe *Dookie* fits you after all!"

Chapter One

Before I dive into the story of how I got the nickname Dookie, a story that is still widely shared amongst residents in my hometown of Spokane, Washington, I think it's only fair that I help define what the term "Dookie" really means, so we are all on the same page.

Some of you may not be hip to the actual meaning of the word. Perhaps it has been too long since you've heard it. Odds are that your parents used that term when they potty trained you: "C'mon! Yoooou can doooo it! Take a dookie! Thaaat's right! Go dookie! Dookie time! Dassagood baby, baby go dooookie all by his self!"

Now are we starting to remember? Great, let's move on.

I should have told my mom that my stomach was acting up again. Once, when I was about six years old, I had this really bad Sloppy Joe sandwich and was sent to the school nurse. The nurse told me it was indigestion, but when I got home I was able to play it off like it was some recurring stomach pain. For years I often used this excuse with my mom to get out of class and stay home. This was one day when I should have faked a bleeding ulcer and skipped the try-outs.

However, my trying out for the Sacajawea Junior High wrestling team was something my father would be proud of. I remembered the conversations we'd had in his back yard while we tossed the pigskin back and forth. He always said things like, "Use your size to your advantage" and "Boy, if I was as big as you I'd be working toward my basketball scholarship right about now."

The thing was, I lived with my mom for most of my younger years. I'm not so certain that this, in itself, was a problem; I just learned how to bake a nice casserole and make my bed rather than play good defense or slam dunk a basketball. At the awkward age of fourteen all I could dunk were donuts. I swear I had a two-inch vertical leap.

Still, I wanted to impress my father, whom I visited every weekend after my parents separated. I figured he'd be excited to see that I was attempting to utilize my untapped strength.

Wrestling was something I thought I'd be good at.

My teenage years were my most heavy years. I clocked in at about three hundred pounds back then. Pinning someone to the mat would be one way of "using my size to my advantage."

Even with my obviously overpowering stature, I still had to weigh in. According to the official wrestling codebook, I was required to find out what weight category I fit into. Incredible as it may seem, a lard butt like myself was not allowed to wrestle someone who weighed 130 pounds.

As a circle of naked jocks sat on the other end of the locker room, playing bloody knuckles while waiting for the coach to arrive, I sat on the bench near the coach's office listening to my cassette walkman and wearing Ray Ban Wayfarer sunglasses.

This was my virtual "do not disturb" sign. When I hid behind those dark shades and the headphones, I felt safe. It was there that I would let the outside world move on without me while I created my own universe in my head, assisted by groups like Public Enemy and Run DMC. The sunglasses were especially helpful since I didn't want to make eye contact and potentially cause static with the troublesome team members.

I isolated myself this way more often, as a teen, than when I was in grade school. It was true that I loved music, but I was also going through a very awkward time in my young life.

In grade school, I had been much more outgoing. I was everyone's favorite class clown, always the prankster. Even in kindergarten I made the kids laugh. This was my constant goal, according to my mother, who said that just before I entered kindergarten, I fretted, saying, "How am I going to entertain these people?"

However, I quickly learned that my elementary comedic social skills were not up to junior high humor standards. Apparently eighth grade teenagers don't find whoopee cushions, spicy chewing gum and Chinese finger traps as funny as my sixth grade friends did. This was one reason why I was an outcast of Sacajawea Junior

High.

I especially did not fit in with the jocks. In fact, it was clear that they absolutely hated me. While their lives revolved around defensive plays and cheerleaders, mine revolved around drama class and the secret hidden levels of Super Mario Brothers.

We did have one thing in common, though: a love for pretty girls. What male teenager with newly developed pubescent hormones doesn't love them? However, my interest centered on one specific girl.

Rachel. Rachel Meyers. She was the most beautiful eighth grader in Sacajawea Junior High. It was her long dark hair that awed me most: the way she would confidently flip it over her ears, the healthy shine that would gleam under the classroom fluorescents.

Though I was a year ahead of her, I took the same math class as she. I sat behind her each day in Algebra, and had a hard time concentrating on anything but her.

I was afraid to ask what made her hair smell so good. Heck, I was afraid to say anything to her at all! I doubted if she even knew I was in the same class as she. I think the only time she ever acknowledged my existence in junior high was when she turned around to give me an evil stare because I laughed too hard after one of Eddie's burps from the back of the classroom. My best friend was always a troublemaker.

She was another reason I decided to take up a sport. I had noticed that she liked the athletic type. So even though the jocks didn't greet me with open arms, I tried to mimic them.

I looked down at my Swatch watch. The coach was apparently running late.

As we waited for his arrival, the other boys prepared for the weigh-in. This process required that we strip down to either our bare selves or wear our underwear so that the coach's assistant could get accurate measurements. A majority of the registrants did not hesitate to strip and had no shame in walking around naked. I, on the other hand, being the underdeveloped teenager that I was (keyword: *was*), chose to postpone the disrobing until the last second, and to strip down to my underwear and no less.

I checked my watch against the wall clock. Yes, he was late. I then looked across the room to see the circle of jocks laughing and pointing at me. What? WHAT? Did I have a boog hanging? I wiped my nose but their laughs grew louder over the music in my headphones.

I turned around to see Ricky Snell (a.k.a. First All-American Wise Guy) wrapped in a towel, dancing and lip-syncing to the song playing in my ears:

C'mon let's sweat! Baby!
Let the music take control...
Let the rhythm moooove yooooou...

I pulled my headphones down around my neck. The giggling hushed so they could hear my reply. "Ricky, glad you're here. Tell me, who sings this song? I forget."

"Idiot. It's C&C Music Factory."

"Ah, right. Thanks." I put the headphones over my ears again. "Keep it that way."

Ricky grabbed my shoulder and twisted me off the bench to the floor. His friends joined him, circling me. Ricky stood above me. I could see what was underneath his towel.

Thank goodness, the coach finally arrived to save me from these naked abusers.

"Line up! Everybody! Line up!"

Ricky ripped the sunglasses off my face and glared at me. "Next time, Aaron, the coach may not be around to save you. You're lucky this time. But when you least expect it..."

"Traylor! Get undressed! Get in line."

There I was, moments later, standing in a line of sweaty, antagonistic, and completely exposed athletes. Ricky and his crew stood behind me and I could feel them burning holes through my head. The coach put the first kid on the scale, moved the little weights to calculate his mass, and began to write his weight down on his clipboard, only to find that his ballpoint had run out of ink.

"Everyone stay where you are. I'm going to get another pen out of the office. I'll be right back."

I remembered Ricky's threat: "When you least expect it...." But I figured he and his boys were smart enough not to do anything to me in the short time while the coach was gone. Before I could turn around, however, to monitor their actions, I experienced a sharp pain to my backside. I looked down to see that my feet had left the ground. The pain increased as I was hoisted upward.

It occurred to me, as I dangled in the air, that I had fallen victim to the mother of all wedgies.

Mind you, it took five strong boys to lift my gargantuan body. Two held one side of my BVD waistband, two more held the other. Ricky had the honor of grasping the backside and proceeded to move his hands up and down in a flossing, yet chafing, motion.

Though I might have defended myself against a flick behind the ear or a charley horse to the leg, nothing, and I mean *nothing*, could have prepared me for this.

My body resorted spontaneously to the only defense mechanism it could muster on short notice.

I defecated.

And not just on myself; I pummeled them, as well.

I'm not talking solids here, folks. I'm talking the Sloppy Joes from the night before...kind of, well, you know...I guess the only word that describes it would be "spackled." I *spackled* the jocks with my own feces.

In an instant, I was tossed to the cold locker room floor.

The mocking laughter had turned to sounds of panic and shock, much like five secretaries trapped inside a high-rise elevator. Horror etched their faces, followed by sheer fury.

The next thing I knew, I was picked up again by the malodorous posse and thrown over their shoulders. They carried me toward the swinging gymnasium entrance doors as I thrashed about to break free of their slippery clutches. But, I was powerless against their combined strength.

I began to scream, at last breaking loose from Ricky's stool-stained hands and arms, only to find that I was too late to grab a door handle to keep myself in the locker room. The door had been kicked open and I was thrust out onto the gym floor, where I slid across the newly varnished basketball court.

As my body came to a screeching halt, I rubbed my legs to ease the pain of the floor burn. While I gathered myself together and shot up to scamper back inside, I heard more laughter. This time it wasn't coming from the locker room. It came from the cheerleading squad, which, prior to my grand entrance, had been practicing their routine for tomorrow afternoon's pep rally.

"Ha! Look! Look everyone! Aaron dookied himself! Ha! Hahaahahaa!!" the team leader giggled as I darted toward the locker room door. To my horror, it was held shut by the jocks behind it.

Also to my horror, Rachel was amidst the hysterically amused cheerleaders.

But, she was the only one who wasn't laughing. She covered her eyes as I covered my chest and crossed my legs, all the while looking for the nearest escape route.

The closest exit led to the parking lot. Once outside, I saw the school buses parked alongside the building. I dared not board one of them, but crouched between them and the wall long enough to catch my breath.

I needed a place to hide, somewhere off campus. I chose the post office directly across the street. Heading that way, I ran into the bathroom and locked the door behind me. I yelled from inside the restroom for the postman to call my mom and have her pick me up.

****

I never returned to Sacajawea Junior High. I simply couldn't. But, though I never set foot in the school again, the Legend of Dookie soon grew to mythic proportions.

Yes, the Legend of Dookie is a tale that continues to be passed from one generation of Sacajawea Junior High students to the next, even to this day.

I remember thinking to myself back then that this was the part I'd have to leave out when I told my dad I'd tried out for a sport.

Thaaat's right! Go dookie!

Dookie time!

Dassagood baby, baby go dooookie all by his self!

Yes. Yes, I did.

Chapter Two

Saturday nights in Spokane, Washington, are also legendary...for boredom. When you are nineteen years old, your entertainment options are severely limited.

I had now graduated from high school. I was living on my own, in my mother's Spokane house. Since she had remarried and moved to Montana, she let me live there as long as I was enrolled at the local community college.

Usually Rachel and Eddie would arrive at my house early in the evening, we'd order a pizza, then spend the rest of the night discussing what we should do to entertain ourselves. By the time we decided, it was usually too late to do anything, or we had talked ourselves into staying in.

As a final resort, we would most often just sit around and jam out to Johnny Styles, night jock for radio station 97.3 "The X."

The X was the coolest station in Spokane, the jocks were hip, the music cutting edge, and the Friday Night Free-For-All request show was interactive fun. Though it was dang near impossible to get through to talk to Johnny, the phone lines being jammed with kids wanting to get their music and voices on the air, I spent many a weekend night on the couch, pressing redial.

"Aaron, you gonna help us figure out what we're going to do tonight?" Rachel said, tossing half a pizza crust at me. "Or are you going to sit there for the next four hours calling in to that radio show? That Johnny guy will probably hang up on you like he always does, anyway. If you're not a chick, you won't get his attention."

Rachel and I had grown to be friends since that fateful day at Sacajawea. I think she took pity on me. When a person accidentally defecates all over his entire junior high wrestling team, he needs all the guidance and support he can get. Both Eddie and Rachel saw me through that traumatizing period.

However, Rachel only hung with us whenever she wasn't dating someone else. To her, I was the "cute boy." Much to my dislike, not the "cute boyfriend," just the "cute boy." She merely tolerated Eddie. It seemed that lately she and I had been serving more as babysitters than as friends to Ed. His drug experimenting was starting to ruin our usually fun times together.

"Yo, dude, check it," said Eddie, tossing a crumpled piece of paper onto my greasy napkin. "I found this tucked away in my wallet."

It was a crudely typed flyer with the word "RAVE" highlighted, along with that day's date and a voice mail number.

"Oh! I've heard about this kind of party!" said Rachel, tugging the flyer out of my hands.

"Rave...Isn't that some kind of a punk mosh concert? I heard they can get kinda wicked, people handin' out free drugs and stuff," replied Eddie as he reached for the last slice of pizza.

"I'm not sure what they are," Rachel said. "I just heard that you're supposed to dance a lot at these. My friends in Seattle told me about them. Let's go check it out."

She got her coat and started applying lipstick to her pretty lips.

I never was the dancing type, but I was always up for something new and different. Besides, it wasn't very often that something different came through our slow town. Since I already had the phone in hand, I called the number to get more info.

"Yeah, why not?" said Eddie. "Beats the same four walls around here. I'm startin' to fry anyway."

"Let's scope it out. I'll drive," offered Rachel. "Eddie, you sit in the back."

****

As we turned the corner, a massive line of teenagers and young adults stretched along one side of the downtown Masonic temple. All the people seemed to have a few apparel choices in common. Girls had cartoony eyeliner and make-up pasted on their faces and clips holding hair back so it wouldn't get in the way of their dancing. Many wore oversized clothing, Adidas shoes and hip bags. Some teenyboppers even had baby pacifiers on cords hanging from their necks!

After waiting a good thirty minutes and paying the three-dollar admission, we stepped into the dark, fog-filled building. We surveyed our surroundings and decided on a mutual meeting ground in case we got lost in the wave of bodies crowding through the entrance.

The party was just starting and yet hundreds had already arrived. I recognized many kids from my old high school, most of whom remembered me by the nickname that still haunted me.

Now, for the record, I had never danced. I mean, I had been to dances, but I had never danced. I was always the oversized wallflower who would occasionally check the punchbowl to see if someone had spiked it yet. This time, however, was different.

This room, these people, this music...it was unlike anything I had ever seen, felt, or heard. The lasers and hazers, the blistering wall of sound, the energy coming from the sweaty dance floor...This was a party! This was something I could groove to!

The music was very futuristic: electronic vocals, synthetic percussions that would make a drummer's hands fall off, ultra-low frequency bass lines that nearly caused our heads to swell, were all synchronized to a primitive rhythm. Nothing like the Hip-Hop I had grown up with, this music seemed, well...spiritual.

I held no reservations and was no longer self-conscious. Instantly I was lost in the energy of the dance floor. I found myself entering a different plateau with the music. I worked myself so hard into the beat that I felt half hypnotized. My body seemed so alive and full of energy that it was as if my nerves were reaching out and clutching the universe, carrying me away to a different level of consciousness.

Oh, man, just thinking about that moment sends chills through me, even now. What was different was the vibe, unlike anything I had ever felt. A free, unrestricted vibe.

And the DJ...

Wow...the DJ kept tweaking the audience and bringing the music ALMOST to climax, only to pull everyone, including myself, back down. The audience begged the DJ to cut the suspense with screams and whistle blowing, but he kept messing with their minds and teasing their senses. In no way was this man going to let them off easy.

This was harmonic foreplay and the crowd surrendered into a vulnerable state that allowed him to have his way with them. We could read his intentions all over his face, which curled up into a dark grin. His suggestive body movements synchronized with the beats permeating the steamy air, a fog-filled atmosphere so laden with perspiration that it was hard to breathe.

Many dancers crammed close to the turntables to witness the amazing performance of scratches laid over funky bass riffs resulting from the quick release and back-cue of the record by the DJ's left hand. He deftly morphed the sounds coming off of each dub plate, and the more pressure he applied to a scratch, the more noise warped out of the speakers. When he'd drop in a sound from the record he was cueing up in his headphones, it was dead on accurate, as if it were part of the record that was playing out of the enormous speakers.

These were not ordinary turntables. I later learned that this specific set of tables had been an industry standard for nearly thirty years. The Technics 1200 turntables' ability to speed up and slow down a record this quickly and accurately made them the choice among DJs worldwide.

No matter what any musician tells you, the 1200s ARE a musical instrument. Anyone can push "play" on a CD and "rewind" and "fast-forward" on a car stereo or home entertainment system. But it takes just as much skill to match and remix record beats as it does to play a guitar.

This DJ was matching beats, blending one song into the next with amazing accuracy, all the while scratching and throwing in sound samples to add flair to his set.

I had no idea, at the time, that LP records were still being made, much less for this purpose. But what he was doing with them had me so intrigued, I was in awe of him. How a person could have so much control of an audience astounded me. This DJ put any rock band I had seen to shame. His performance was more energetic, louder and much more cutting edge than anything that had entertained prior audiences in this town. This was something totally new to me, something I was determined to know more about.

For the rest of the night and into the morning, I danced next to friends and cared not how I danced or how they expressed themselves. I looked into the eyes of complete strangers and felt I totally related to them without saying a word. I finally opened up and began to converse with my ex-schoolmates, who all seemed to feel the same way I did.

Then and there I came to a conclusion regarding what it was that united us all that night, and what would become our common destiny: we all shared a bond, I believed - young, old, male, female, of any race, creed, religion.

I later found out that this bond has a name among ravers: P.L.U.R. (PEACE, LOVE, UNITY, RESPECT). My life, I believed, had been forever changed because of it; my only regret was that it had taken me nineteen years to learn of this...

I finally caught up with Eddie, who was stressing out about trying to find his backpack, which he had misplaced somewhere in the building. He soon recalled where he had left it, in the same place that we were all supposed to meet if we got lost.

We thought it was too cool that it had been surrounded by hundreds of teenagers for hours, and wasn't even touched!

****

Early morning arrived fast. I found myself in deep philosophical conversation and group backrub sessions in the "chill room," a toned down place to relax, with mellow, vibey music, pale lighting, water trays and fruity scented incense formulated to calm nerves and usher in your second, third, or fourth wind.

I was utterly spent when it came time to go. I rustled up Eddie and found Rachel off in a corner of the building, batting her long eyelashes at the DJ, who was surrounded by curious and talkative followers. She motioned for us to meet her out at the car and dug into her pocket for a pen to write her number on the DJ's hand.

Making the adjustment to sunlight was difficult, but by the time my eyes completely focused, I could see that as the rave was letting out, so was the church across the street. I noticed the people and families all dolled up in their Sunday best, filing out of the cathedral, faces bright with newfound inspiration that would carry them through their week.

Until I moved out on my own, I had been to church all my life. In fact, Eddie and I first met as toddlers in the Sunday School where my parents and his grandfather attended. His grandpa had raised him after his mother abandoned him, and after my folks broke up, mother continued to take me to church every Sunday.

Thinking back, I guess I had a pretty strong faith as a little guy. And I must have loved music, even then, because my childish form of worship included singing "Jesus Loves Me" to the neighbor's geese down the alley. Mom tells me I used to take my tricycle down the lane and sit behind the neighbor's fence, crooning this assurance to my feathery audience:

Jesus loves me, this I know,
For the Bible tells me so;
Little ones to Him belong;
They are weak, but He is strong.

I was apparently heedless of what any kids in the surrounding yards might think, a characteristic I did not carry into adolescence.

I stopped attending church once Mom moved to Montana. As I got older, I was not as passionate for the faith as she was. Sorry, Mom, but I just wasn't feeling it. By then, I hated that kind of singing and worship and I could barely stay awake during the sermons.

But, even though I neglected organized religion, I still believed in God. I may not have known Him like my Mom did, but I felt He would reveal Himself to me when the time was right.

Looking back, I see now that I was stubborn. If He wanted me to get to know Him, I figured He was going to have to introduce Himself to me by means of life experiences rather than through stories from the pulpit.

Today, as I walked out into the daylight and observed the families leave their church, I figured I was just as fulfilled as they. I believed that this gathering I had just attended had truly introduced me to God in ways they couldn't imagine.

The music I had just experienced was about to become my religion.

Just what that would mean, down the line, I could never have anticipated.

Chapter Three

That day, when I tried to rest, I couldn't achieve much needed sleep. The few times I drifted off, my thoughts went a million miles a second, causing me to have vivid daydreams.

The lights and sounds from the rave had really done a number on my senses. Blurs of multicolored globes had burned into my retinas and my ears still hummed from dancing too close to the speakers. My body felt numb.

I decided that since it was one of the first sunny days of summer, I would give up trying to sleep and have Rachel drop me off at Riverfront Park, to enjoy the peace of our city's largest recreational site. Walking helps me calm myself and I enjoy a little alone time every so often. This would be the perfect place for me to reflect on the party that had "forever changed my life."

My entire perspective on life in general had been altered. In the most unlikely of places, I had come to terms with the way my life was shaping up, and I had concluded that I wasn't satisfied.

As I walked through the park, all I did was think about myself and my future. What was my true calling? You know…the deep stuff. The only thing I did know was that I wanted more than what I had.

I made my way down a winding trail leading to a cliff that overlooks the roaring rapids of the beautiful Spokane River, which cuts right through downtown. I had heard of the rocky protrusion called "Inspiration Point," but I had never before visited it. How odd that I had come upon it, today of all days.

Many had been here before me. Initials and graffiti were carved into the overgrown lilac trees along the trail. I was almost hit in the face by protruding branches as I narrowly trekked down the cobblestone.

Upon entering the viewpoint, I found a stone bench and sat down. I closed my eyes and drifted away to the hypnotizing sounds of the crashing rapids below. I invited the mist from the high waves to caress my sensitive face.

I had found a measure of peace, when, all at once, it felt as if the mist became colder and heavier. I peeked one eye open to see that a very small, dark rain cloud had formed right over the courtyard. A strange rain lasted for only a fleeting moment and then the cloud dissipated abnormally fast. It was as if a dark force had tried to take up a fight against the brighter horizon, in a battle it couldn't win.

Suddenly, something spoke to me there on the rock. Something unexplainable, yet comforting. Something supernatural. When I spoke, I received a reply in my mind. This spooked me. I questioned what kind of spirit I was talking to and I seemed to receive a reassuring answer.

I began to wonder if sleep deprivation might have tapped into some weird circuitry upstairs. Perhaps I should return when I was fully rested, I thought. But first, I needed answers.

This mysterious voice talked to me in my own tongue, nothing riddled or complex. No confusing foreshadowing. We spoke as if I were talking to a long distance friend over the phone. When I asked questions, I received answers.

Right then and there, I believed, my destiny had been chosen.

My thoughts reverted back to where I had been a few hours before. I envisioned myself on stage at the Masonic Temple, instead of that other DJ. And instead of hundreds like last night, thousands of screaming dancers were mesmerized by my movements behind the 1200s. All the while Rachel was draped over my shoulder, rooting me on.

I wanted to be like the DJ I had seen last night. I wanted his glory and recognition. His talent, his stirring music.

I was going to be a DJ!

"But why stop there?" the mysterious voice asked.

The title DJ is a very flexible label. There are turntable DJs like the one I had experienced the night before. And then there are radio DJs who announce on the air.

Suddenly, my mind flashed to the many times I had heard cocky Johnny Styles strutting his verbal stuff over the airwaves.

Wow! I thought. *Could I ever hold Spokane radio listeners in the palm of my hand, like despicable but oh-so-cool Mr. Styles?*

It seemed the unseen presence nudged me.

"Sure, why not?" I said aloud. "I know music as well as any of these guys!"

I let myself imagine me in both worlds, radio and club. In my fantasy, I handled turntables and microphones with the finesse of a juggler.

All at once I knew...I was going to succeed with both!

Chapter Four

When I walked into 97.3 "The X" FM, I saw on the walls many photos of people whom I had known only as radio voices. *Wow,* I thought to myself. *What a bunch of ugly guys!*

Most of these pictures proved why these people were behind microphones and not on television screens. They looked like those guys in high school who sat far in the back of the classroom. With their long hippy hair, unshaven faces, torn rock tees, bleached jeans, and with their headphones cranked, blaring blistering metal tunes, they usually sat throwing their heads around to the music, ignoring the world.

So this is where all the dudes that hang out in smoker's alley find jobs when they graduate, I thought. Then I realized that these guys did have one advantage over me. They had gone straight from high school to the radio world and had years of experience. Though I was in college, it would take me a long time to catch up with them. Hopefully, I at least looked better than they. I had managed to snatch up some really cool hand-me-down suits from the Salvation Army thrift store. I was stylin' and felt good about myself. Maybe this self-confidence would be noticed by the program director, and he would see potential in such an eager-to-learn beginner.

"Mr. Styles will be right with you," the secretary said. She must have noticed that I caught a peek at my watch for the third or fourth time. "He is always really busy, you understand. Nervous?" she asked.

"Me? Nahhh. I'm cool," I replied, twitching my left leg and biting my thumbnail.

"Just relax. That polyester suit will definitely score some points with the big man," she said with a wink. "You raided your old pop's closet, didn't you?"

I blushed and tucked my head into a radio trade magazine.

Boisterous talk filled the hallway leading from the main lobby. I recognized that hearty voice and those bellowing guffaws from the airwaves of Spokane's largest Top 40 station. It was "Mr." Johnny Styles, the hottest night show jock in the city. He sounded like a cocky, self-obsessed punk on the air, but, man, I listened to his show every night. There was no competition in this big little city; he knew it and wasn't afraid to express that fact to his audience. People, mostly young adults, would call his show to request music, all the while knowing that they would be subjected to degrading put downs live on the air. The audience loved it when Johnny chewed up his callers and simply spit them out. Once, he even made a little twelve-year-old break down and start bawling just because he had innocently requested Billy Ray Cyrus during the R&B countdown.

"Oh, that must be him. He just returned from his lunch break," said the secretary. "I'll let him know you're here to see him."

I certainly hoped that this dude's on-air personality was just a front, but if I'd known he would be the one to interview me, I never would have shown up! Too late now.

"Who? What? Aaron, huh? Yeah, yeah. Hang on a minute," groaned Johnny behind his closed office door. His voice carried like a trumpet.

The secretary came out of his office with Johnny close behind. "You Aaron Traylor?" he asked, as he flipped through a stack of CD singles in his arms.

"Ahem, yeah, er, yes sir…" I humbly replied, standing at attention.

"Sit down. I'll be with you soon," he said without making eye contact, and, re-entering his office, slammed the door behind him.

The secretary smiled lamely and offered me a doughnut.

"I'm fine. Not hungry, thanks." I sat back and read the same trade mag for the third time.

Forty-five minutes later Johnny came out his office and looked at me in shock. "You still here? Forgot you were waiting. Want a doughnut?"

"No. Not hungry, thanks," I replied again.

"Your loss, partner. I'll be right back," he said, aiming toward the exit.

"Um, with all due respect, sir, I have been waiting here for over an hour-and-a-half," I interjected. "I'm not interested in a pastry nor am I really fond of reading the same radio business magazine over and over. I have come here for an internship and I am told to see you about this. Will you please give me five minutes of your time? I'll make it as painless as possible."

Johnny glared at me, up one side and down the other. The silence was brutal. "Well?" I asked.

"I was going to buy that exact same jacket at the thrift store just the other day," he said with a smirk.

****

I sat among gold records and rock star autographed pictures. I held back a smile at seeing a framed photo on his wall, showing him shaking Billy Ray Cyrus' hand.

"So..." Johnny mumbled while going over my resume. "Says here you got jack to contribute to this station. I'm supposed to be impressed by this?"

I scurried for a retort. "Uh...well, yeah, but ..."

Nice one, Aaron.

Before I had a chance to come up with a respectable reply, I was thrown off track when Johnny lit an incense stick with his left hand and unrolled a baggy of bud with his right hand!

"Fresh from the college scene, huh? Think you got what it takes to hang with the big boys? What you got to offer me, man?" he challenged.

After a painfully long moment of dead air, I responded, "I believe that whatever you throw my way, I'll be able to cut it out just like the rest of you fellas." My eyes didn't move from the nonchalant motions of his hands as he rolled a fat joint in front of me, obviously heedless of my opinion.

"What you wanna be, some superstar DJ? 'Cause we here can't stand for that. Ain't got room for Don Imus wannabes. You here to get some females? Let me tell ya something, boy. Ninety percent of all female listeners are fat, food stamp usin', trailer park livin', white trash. They all got sexy voices, but once you meet em' you'd be like HELP!"

He sparked his doob and continued.

"Look, you've come here with nothing for me. I don't like taking chances…" he hacked "…on some punk kid poser tryin' to be the next thing 'round here."

After a few enormous tokes from the skank weed, he offered me some.

What was I to do? I mean, for the record, I had never hit up weed in my life! But, here I was with the chance to score really big with a potentially exciting career. Should I accept his offering?

Without a second thought I reached for the roach.

"You, on the other hand, there's something different about you," Johnny said. "What's your radio name gonna be?"

Chapter Five

Now don't get me wrong. Despite the fact that I was wearing a previously used Easter bunny rental costume around my hometown, I was very excited to be considered part of the team for the largest radio station in the Inland Empire. I felt as if things were finally starting to take shape in my life and my destiny was beginning to unfold, even if it did mean that, for the time being, I had to represent the station as an enormous bunny mascot. I mean seriously...this costume...couldn't they at least have found me one that fit? The pink, furry legs extended only to my lower thighs, exposing my hairy knees!

As I paraded around Riverfront Park, passing out station bumper stickers, I assured myself that I would soon be able to reveal my true identity on the air with pride. I'd be just like "big boy" Johnny, who seemed to enjoy the attention he got from radio groupies who followed him everywhere.

There he was, now, sitting in the station booth at the arts and crafts show, signing autographs and dissing teenagers. Young ladies giggled and whispered into each other's ears while Johnny indulged in flirtatious conversation. He wasn't the most attractive guy around, but his confidence and smooth, street-wise talk made the girls melt like butter.

And there I was, dealing with rug rats and ogling parents. Most little kids feared my overwhelming size. With rabbit ears protruding out of my head, I had to be at least eight feet tall! You can imagine that when I bent down to hug the children, most of them ran in the opposite direction, or began to bawl and tucked themselves behind their parents' legs.

When it came teenagers, they got their kicks out of playing a game called "Make the Big Bunny Fall!" There were times when I would just be standing there and some kid would come up as if to hug me, then throw all of his weight into me, causing me to fall over another punk's back as he knelt behind me.

That got old real quick.

On top of all of this, it was insanely hot inside that costume of synthetic fur, as the spring sun beat down. I think I was the only person in the park who wished it was still winter. For the first time in my life, I felt claustrophobic; it was hard to breathe and I began to feel faint.

Was this Johnny's way of testing my stamina? It seemed I was in the beginning stages of radio boot camp and this was "hell week." I imagined that Sergeant Johnny would rather I not succeed in this business, and was bent on humiliating me into quitting the first week. Looking back, I think he only wanted to see if I could hold up my end of the bargain and cut it just like the "big boys."

Putting all of that aside in the interest of my destiny, I chose to continue until all of the bumper stickers in my hand were distributed.

I had only a hundred or so to go, so it would only be a short while until I could take a breather in the air-conditioned station vehicle with the tinted windows.

I couldn't help but notice, even with the limited vision through the mask, that Inspiration Point was only a stone's throw away. I figured that the hopes raised there were being answered. This inspired me to press forward and accomplish my grueling task.

Johnny's live broadcast echoed throughout the park from the booth's monitors: "97.3 'The X' FM, Today's hottest music. Johnny Styles live at Riverfront Park for the Eighth Annual Arts and Crafts Show. Come on down and check out local artists' displays and, please, help welcome our newest addition to 'The X' family: Dookie the Bunny! Tell me, Dookums, how did you get your name, anyway? Ha!"

Johnny pointed the microphone in my direction. Now believe me, I tried for the life of me to avoid becoming one of Johnny's targets of ridicule. But, I simply could not talk! My voice was non-existent due to dehydration!!

"Seems like the ol' Dookster isn't too talkative today. All right, listen up everybody, I've gotta CD and a coupon for a free slurpee if someone gives our new mascot a wedgie! Ha HA HAA!!"

I walked away and continued to dole out the remainder of the stickers, becoming increasingly weaker as I rushed to finish my duties.

****

"MOMMY! Look, the Easter bunny! MOMMY!!" cried out a child's voice. If it were not for the bunny head constricting my peripheral vision, I would have been able to prepare for the sudden attack of affection from a small girl. The short, blond bundle of joy wrapped herself around my perspiring leg and proceeded to nuzzle her nose up against the pink fur.

"Oh, quick, honey! Snap a picture of this! Look at her. Isn't that adorable?" shrilled the excited mom as she rushed to the scene.

"Sorry, if you wouldn't mind standing in the shade, the missus would like me to take a picture of you and our daughter!" said the father, equipped with one of those cheesy "forgot the camera at home" disposable tourist snapshot dealies.

"Shade! Yea boy!" I thought to myself, and proceeded toward the nearest set of lilac trees. Problem was, the kid was still glued to my left leg. Was it my sticky sweat that kept her lodged to my thigh, or the fact that she had never had her hands on such a large stuffed animal before?

"Can we keep him?" asked the child.

Having this much extra baggage on my body, while attempting to move toward cooler temperatures, was overtaxing any stamina I had left. I could barely utter a plea for help, as I attempted to dislodge the little girl. My eyes rolled back in my head. I saw nothing but darkness. Had it not been for the little one holding my weight to the ground, I would have collapsed!

Let's consider this little girl's point of view for a moment, shall we? Here we have an innocent child, no older than three, thrilled beyond her wildest fantasies by what could possibly have been the largest bunny ever. It was my duty to spread joy and love to the young ones, but instead, I began to vomit all over her pretty flowered overalls.

Rumor has it that the girl was so emotionally scarred by this ordeal that her parents had to hide her Peter Cottontail, Roger Rabbit and Bugs Bunny stuffed animals until she was fourteen.

"Today's hot music! 97.3 'The X' FM! Once again Johnny Styles here live at the Eighth Annual Arts and Crafts Show in the park on a beautiful spring day! Stop by and visit us at 'The X booth' and...holy! Look! Dookie upchucked all over that little girl's drawers!"

From that day forth I had acquired another legendary nickname: "Dookie-the Pukey-Bunny."

Chapter Six

After hours of practically bathing in Lemon Ice Gatorade in the comfort of my air conditioned apartment, I was due for a celebration. I kept thinking, as an ice pack dribbled down my blistered face, "I am a radio broadcasting network's gofer bunny boy! I fear no man, for I am now a vital part of society! If anyone gets in the way of my destiny and dreams...why, I'll either defecate, or project vomit on my detractors!"

My first *tour de force* was to sign up for my very own cell phone, just to show how sophisticated I had become!

Time to rally up my homeboy. I had pre-programmed Eddie's cell number into my auto dial.

"What up," said Eddie, answering the phone before the first ring finished.

"It's Friday night," I replied. "Bring some beers over."

"I'm down. Where's the ladies at tonight? Gotta get my groove on. My back is feeling mighty strong tonight."

"Beats me. Let's cruise Riverside in your Audi."

"Na, some fool jacked my hood ornament. Can't be seen driving 'round like dat." Eddie paused briefly. "Hold up, I was just scoping through my wallet to count my wad and came across this flyer for that new club 'The Jungle.'" Eddie was always so down with every crew in town that he would get the know-how or invite to all the coolest hang-outs before anyone else I knew.

"Another flyer, eh? We gotta call another one of them numbers to find out where it's at and what's up," I replied.

"Ain't nuttin like one of dem raves we been to. Says here this is a club of sorts. All ages. Hip-Hop DJ: The Shaman. Heh, what kinda DJ name is that? He must be up there to have a high and mighty name like 'The Shaman,'" Eddie repeated.

"Hmm, sounds like that's the place to be," I replied.

"OOH! Hey, yo, hold up G! Says here it's ladies' night. Ooooh baby, and the feeling's right, oh what a night!"

"Work it, dog! I'll see ya tonight. Don't forget the brew!" I said, unsure that he had caught the tail end of the sentence before hanging up.

****

The Hip-Hop music didn't seem to please the gutter punks that we had to snake between to get to the entrance of Club Jungle.

"Spare any change man?" seemed to be the most popular phrase uttered by these low life degenerates. And it's not like they were asking for money for door admission. Eddie and I cut through the crowd with our eyes lowered and pockets covered.

We entered the establishment, whose daytime front was a fully functional dance-training academy. It was hard to miss the framed pictures of the guy who was taking our door money, which showed him decked out in tight leotards, doing aerial splits. What was also very noticeable were the displays of huge trophies received from area dance competitions. Beyond the lobby, black scrim was duct taped to the walls, giving a dark, club-like atmosphere to the interior.

"Man, we better watch ourselves here," Eddie said. "God knows if we hit on any of these chickies we will be slapped with a statutory, cradle robbin' rap! Worse yet, some big daddy is gonna come whup us for taking off a piece of his daughter!"

"Yeah, it's hard to tell the older ones from the pups nowadays," I said, as we stared down the adjacent hallway which was lined with mirrors and leg stretching bars for ballet practice. One slender girl was flexing her strong calves across a pole, her back turned to us. Our eyes trained in on her amazing qualities like homing radar.

"Yo, check that little Betty, for example. She gotsta be fourteen, knowing our luck," said Eddie.

"No, too tall for that age. Besides, I would recognize that backside anywhere!"

Eddie focused, "HOO YEA BABY! Yo, whaaaat up, Rachel!"

"Figured you guys would be here on Ladies' Night, of all nights," she said, curling her torso around to make eyes at us.

"I figured you would be out struttin' your stuff with Mr.

33

Superstar rave DJ, tonight," I chuckled as I approached her. "You did get his number, didn't you?"

"I left messages at his house but he never called me back. Doesn't matter. I've got my eyes set on someone else, now," Rachel said in a sultry tone.

Unfortunately, she didn't mean yours truly. She was staring over my shoulder at the DJ booth raised above the dance floor.

"Come up here, I want you to meet the man of my dreams," she cooed.   "Looking forward to it," I mumbled.

****

Rachel and I wrapped around the elevated booth, leaving Eddie behind, and approached the top of the steps leading to the control room. "Oh, Mister Shaman!" purred Rachel.

I had to admit, not to sound fruity or anything, but Rachel did have good taste when it came to the opposite sex. This Shaman fella looked as if he had jumped out of a men's swimsuit catalog and behind a pair of turntables. He was in perfect physical shape, as evidenced by the rippled definitions beneath his tight tee shirt. Shaman leaned over the mixing board, his left hand still placed on a record platter and a pair of headphones pinched between his head and muscular shoulder, to acknowledge Rachel's beckoning.

"I would like you to meet my friend, Dookie," she said.

"'Sup, man?" he said with a sincere smile, obviously too busy mixing to carry on a conversation.

"Would you mind if she and I just stood out of the way and watched you in action?" I asked, admiring his graceful talent.

"Grab a seat and enjoy the ride, man!" said Shaman, as he once again focused on his duties of hyping the audience.

Rachel leaned over the mixing table, resting her chin on her hands and batting her deep blue eyes at Shaman. "I sure love the way your hands move," she flirted.

Shaman acted as if he didn't hear what she said and continued to mix, with a satisfied grin.

He seemed to really enjoy what he was doing. He was truly skilled on the decks. His fluid motions with the record and the mixer's cross fader produced some seriously wicked beats. The cool thing about his music was that it always seemed to have a recognizable vocal track, like KRS One and Arrested Development, laid over a new bass line and samples. These were remixes of the latest Top 40 Hip-Hop, all tricked out with extended mixes, extra long breakdowns and jumpier rhythms than you would hear in the original versions. Stuff like this was never heard on Spokane radio, and was strictly intended for the club scene.

I later learned that Shaman had gone in on half the rent to use this dance studio for a weekend youth nightclub. The seventy-five or so dancers present tonight seemed to be enjoying themselves, singing to recognizable lyrics and grooving to the new beats.

As all this was going on, Rachel remained focused on Shaman's triceps.

"Hey, Rachel, you hear about me getting a job at The X?" I proudly said for both to hear.

"What? Yea, right," Rachel replied, too zoned in on Shaman to look at me.

"Wait, OK, yeah! I knew I heard your name before!" Shaman exclaimed. "Yeah, you were on the local news."

Rachel finally turned her head to look at me. With one eyebrow raised, she asked, "You ...a DJ?"

"Dookie, right? Yeah, Dookie, the Pukey-Bunny!" the Shaman laughed.

Rachel's curious grin turned serious. "Pardon?"

I nervously motioned to Shaman to not elaborate on the whole bunny thing.

"Some dad sold Channel 6 snapshots of a giant rabbit in the park tossing his lunch on his defenseless daughter. They had it on the five o'clock news. Nice to meet you, Mr. Bunny!" said the Shaman, trying to maintain his composure.

Rachel rolled her eyes and aimed her curvaceous hips closer toward Shaman's turntables.

"I'll be out dancing to you, man. See ya 'round," I said, turning glumly away.

"It was good to meet you, Dookie!" said Shaman. "Maybe I'll catch up with you later. I'll be making way for a guest DJ in about half-an-hour."

"Go ahead and make way! I'm here, man," said a sun-glassed fellow holding a case of records at the stage entrance.

"Superstar DJ's in the house," cried Rachel, lunging toward him with her arms wide open.

"Dookie, I would like you to meet Halo. Halo, Dookie, Dookie, Halo," said Shaman.

"What's up?" I said, extending my hand for a shake. I recognized him as the DJ who had played at the first party we attended, the DJ who had inspired my interest in the profession.

To my dismay, he ignored me and brushed my shoulder as he moved toward the mixing table, bumping Shaman out of the way.

"Yeah, yeah. Move out, everybody. I need my space. You! You can stay," Halo grumbled as he grabbed Rachel close to his chest.

Eddie was waiting at the foot of the steps. "Yo, we outty!"

"What? Dude, we just got here!" I said.

"Kill that idea! We going to your house with or without you!" he replied, ushering from beneath his arms a set of buxom girls. "Don't worry, G, I carded them first. They're leeegaal."

"Eddie!" I said, motioning him aside. "Dude, you gotta understand...I made a pact with my mom not to have any guests at my house after 10:00 on any night. She finds out, I'm lunch meat."

"What? Aaron, your mom lives four-hundred miles away in sheepland Montana. She would never know!" he argued.

"It's the whole principle issue, Eddie. She is letting me live there rent free and on my own while she is in-between renters, so I can stay in school. I don't think this is such a good idea," I said sternly.

I paused and stared at the two new beauties who were now dancing together. "Then again..." I sighed, "My mom does seem to be going to bed a bit earlier these days."

"That's the spirit, Holmes! I'll grab my coat and warm up the car," Eddie said, breaking out in a tune. "Oh yes, it's ladies' night and the feelin's right...."

The four of us headed across the dance floor toward the exit doors. Suddenly, all of us, including the floor-full of dancers, were stopped in our tracks by the sound of an air raid horn blaring from the speakers. This was the mood changer for Halo's opening set. Quick, tribal drumbeats caught off-guard the feet and ears of every listener.

Most of the traditional dancers left the floor for a break, which allowed a handful of others the opportunity to break loose and use the whole dance floor.

I wished I could have stayed to re-live memories of the weekend before, but Eddie had already disappeared, and was getting cozy with the blonde, who was sipping on a road beer in his Audi.

Chapter Seven

Eddie and I partied until we puked. There is nothing in the world that can describe the bonding that goes on between two life-long friends sharing the same toilet bowl for rounds of regurgitation.

Picture, if you will, my homeboy and me lying on the linoleum, our clothes drenched in bathroom floor stains, our rosy cheeks pressed against the cool porcelain bowl. Our eyes were red and puffy with blood blisters from all the dry heaving, and tears streaked down our sweaty faces.

"Yo, Ed!" I muttered. "They say that if you don't want a morning hangover you need to drink a shot or a beer as soon as you wake up."

"Fact one," Eddie replied. "it's not morning, it's 1:30 AM. Fact two, we got's no mo' beer. Fact three, I don't *want* anymo' BEER!"

"Where do you suppose the girls ran off to?" I asked.

"Beats me. I figure they busted outta here after they walked in on us pukin' together."

The phone rang from in the living room.

"I ain't gettin'it," mumbled Eddie.

"Who's calling at this time of night? Don't matter, voice mail kicks in after four rings," I groaned.

The ringing ended at only two, followed by the sound of one of the girls answering.

"I thought they left!" I exclaimed.

"Are you decent?" the brunette giggled from the other side of the door. "Some lady called, asking for Aaron. I told her that there is no one here by that name and that this is Dookie's house and he is indisposed at the moment. Suddenly, there was nothing but a dial tone!"

I scrambled toward the living room on my hands and knees to check the caller ID. "Holy...Eddie!" I cried. "MY MOM JUST CALLED!"

"Shall we help you clean up and make your beds? Hey, Cindy, toss me my bra!" said the blonde.

I called my mom's house and received no answer. Call waiting interrupted the continued ringing. I clicked over.

"Hello?"

"Dookie? Johnny. Get down here."

"Wha? Wait, I.."

"Ten minutes. Be here."

Click.

"Everybody! GET OUT OF MY HOUSE!" I screamed while hurdling over Eddie's limp, motionless body toward the bathroom medicine cabinet. "Pepto Bismol? Yup," I said, grabbing the bottle and heading to my bedroom. "Baseball cap? Got it. Keys? In my pocket. New shirt?" I paused to sniff my collar. "GAG! Where's the Old Spice?"

I ushered the girls out the door with me. "Ladies, it's been pleasant. We will call you...Eddie!! Lock up for me and...get out!!"

There was no reply.

I hopped on my motorcycle and peeled around the corner en route to the station. My stomach churned and my head throbbed with every pothole I hit.

****

It's a miracle that I wasn't pulled over for the maniacal way I was driving. My license had not been on the list of things that I figured I needed before I darted out of my house.

The elevator door at the X opened to the fifth floor and I stumbled out, belching and digging through my pocket to find the station key, while squirting shots of Binaca into my sore mouth with the other hand.

Johnny opened the office doors before I was able to unlock them myself. He peeked through the crack. "1:46. You are late. Come in." Johnny proceeded down the hallway to the control room with me trudging behind.

"You ready to cut it like us Big Boys?" he asked.

"Pardon?" I replied.

"Mr. Hi-I'm-a-Dumb-Overnight-DJ-Boy showed up to work drunk. He had ten minutes of dead air while he decided to take a little nap between CDs. I showed up and booted his sorry self out the door. Now you have the honors. CDs are there, program log is here; EBS tone button is under the table. Keep the station on air and you get to keep your job. I'm out."

Johnny pushed me down in front of the control board and slammed the door behind him as he left.

****

In front of me sat THE most ominous and intimidating piece of machinery I had ever encountered. A tall, wide box that contained more dials, switches and knobs than the snotty computer on 2001: A Space Odyssey. My jaw dropped to the floor when I noticed that the song in the CD player had only twenty-five seconds left to play!

Just like I was in a James Bond flick, I feared that if the timer expired before I made the right move, humanity and the world as we know it would burst into flames! I squinted my puffy eyes to put all the blurry bells and hazy whistles into focus.

I managed to identify a slider button labeled "recorder," then I recognized the "microphone" button. Finally, with only seven seconds remaining and the vocals of the song beginning to fade, I saw a button that said "CD 2." Actually, in my besotted condition, I saw three buttons that said CD 2! I aimed for the middle one, held my breath, closed my eyes, and poked my finger at the control board just as the song ended.

The next tune kicked in to play and began to broadcast across the Spokane airwaves!

With a sigh of relief, my exhausted body relaxed. Then, I realized I had only four minutes and twenty seconds until the new song ended to familiarize myself with this foreign piece of equipment. If I were to master the art of cueing those CDs, I would be able to catch myself up to speed.

A rush of adrenaline overtook the pain of the night's festivities. I forgot to be in so much discomfort as everything became clearer to me.

After about an hour of practicing transitions between music and commercials, I was a little less nervous. I began to rehearse aloud what I was going to say for my first-break-ever on the radio!

All of a sudden, a flashing red light caught the corner of my eye. It was the commercial log on the computer screen requesting that we perform an EBS test after the current song was over! Now, for the record, all personnel at a radio station are required by the Federal Communications Commission (FCC) to be thoroughly trained in all national and local emergency news broadcast procedures. I, however, was not.

The EBS introduction automatically began to play on the air after the song ended:

"This   is   a   test   of   the   Emergency   Broadcast System.........................."

"Where is the EBS button again?" I thought to myself, frantically scanning the control room.

"..."

"CDs there, program log here.......AUGH!"

"..."

"Where is the dang tone button?!"

"..."

I said a silent prayer, turned my microphone on and began to emit   a   high-pitched   wavering   tone   from   my   mouth.
"BeeeeEEEEeeeEEEEEeeeeeeeeeeeeeeeEEEEEEEEEEEp!
This has been a test of the Emergency Broadcast System. If this were an actual emergency...."

Seconds later I received a phone call from Johnny on the office hotline. Distant sounds of laughter and socializing echoed behind his drunken voice.

"That's your get out of jail free pass. Next time you won't be so lucky!"

Click!

****

Pulling into my driveway at 8:30 that morning, I saw a large pile of Hefty bags lying in the yard, with my furniture, free for the looting, stacked next to them.

Fortunately, Eddie had kept guard over my belongings as he sat on the porch awaiting my arrival. I didn't need to ask. My mother's rental agency had sent someone to move me out of the house.

"I grabbed everything I could, Holmes," Ed said.

I collapsed on the concrete walk, rubbing my hot forehead into the dewy grass.

After about five minutes of total silence, Eddie pointed out a large utility truck pulling up to the curb. "Here comes my Grampa," he said. "He's here to help us move you into my house until you find a place to stay."

I picked myself off the ground and embraced my best friend. Weak, tired and defenseless, I cried on his shoulder until he pushed me away.

"Wussy..." Eddie nudged my shoulder. "Grab your stuff. Let's roll."

Chapter Eight

Eddie's floor smelled funny. Kinda like foul beer and Cheetos. But at least it was a place to rest my head after I got kicked out of my house.

Before my mother had been gracious enough to let me housesit her Spokane home, Ed's trailer house had been the joint when it came to outrageous house parties. Now, compared to my mom's place, it was a pit. It seemed everyone preferred my house over his.

It had been only a matter of time before things got out of control and my privilege of living there was revoked. (Note to parents: if you live two states away from your child, trusting that he or she will abide by your rules, don't.)

I told myself it didn't matter, though. Always the optimist, I dreamed that it would be only a matter of time until I got back on my feet again. After all, I was on my way to making a name for myself in the radio industry.

Johnny was impressed that I had been able to keep the station afloat the previous weekend, so he scheduled me for the overnight shifts every Friday and Saturday. My days as the Bunny were over. During the week I did sticker stops and research calls for the station, so I would soon be accumulating some good cash. Enough to get my own place again, or to find a roommate with a cleaner house and a bed I could use.

Yes, sleeping on the stained carpet in my best friend's living room was only temporary, I told myself.

Best friends can make horrible roommates. Moving in with someone that you barely know is much better because you are able to establish house rules from scratch and abide by them more easily. On the other hand, if you move in with someone you've known forever, relaxed expectations are already established and habits of interaction are much more difficult to break.

"Yo, man…get up!" Eddie barked, bumping the noisy vacuum cleaner into my head. "Company's coming over."

The vacuum seemed to have a broken belt because all it did

was push the gum wrappers and beer can tabs around my face.

"What time is it?" I grumbled as I shifted my body onto the couch.

"It's time for you to wake up, fool."

"Who is coming over that makes it so important for you to clean house?" I asked.

"DJ Halo. I gave him my number at The Jungle so we could hook up for a few brews and talk about his party."

"His party?"

Eddie flipped the switch on the vacuum so we could talk without yelling. "Yeah, homeboy is gonna throw one of his own raves. I guess he was just spinning at the one we went to. He got inspired and wants to do one himself. I figured you two would hit it off, being in the same field and all."

I remembered how arrogant Halo had been the last time I had seen him. He seemed to have little respect for anyone around him. What could he and I possibly have in common? Except for the fact that we both seemed to admire the same girl.

I wondered what had become of Rachel. She had never called to check in, but then, even if she had, I wouldn't have been home to answer the phone. I supposed it would be a good idea to call her and see how her weekend went.

I always got nervous whenever I tried to call her. I wanted to say things that would impress her, but I would get jittery if even the slightest pause or stutter interrupted our conversation. Eddie told me that I tried way too hard whenever she and I were together and that I should just be myself. It was awfully hard to be myself when I wasn't too comfortable with myself in the first place. When you are close to someone who is very attractive, it's difficult to say the right things, especially when you are as self conscious as I was.

"You gotta call Rachel and let her know where you at now, being you got kicked to the curb and all," Eddie smirked. He had a way of reading what was on my mind without my saying a word. "You should invite her over tonight."

"Nah, she's probably doing homework tonight," I replied, not wanting her to come around when Superstar DJ was stopping by. I knew Rachel really liked confident guys and she had seemed awfully interested in him at The Jungle. The last thing I wanted to do was to put those two in the same room together again.

"I'll give her a call and let her know where I am, though."

I dialed Rachel's number and she answered quickly with that sultry voice of hers.

"Rachel, what's up? It's Aaron."

"Hey, sweetie!" she replied.

Sweetie...sweetie? Rachel had never used that word to describe me before.

"Um, yeah, hey...I just wanted to let you know that..."

"You aren't living at your house anymore," Rachel interrupted. "I noticed! I came over to your house yesterday to see if you were around."

This was odd, I thought. Rachel just doesn't "stop by." It normally took a little coaxing on my end to convince her to come over. What was this all about?

"Yeah, parents found out that I was having parties at their place and they gave me the boot. So why did you come by?" I asked.

"Was that you on The X the other night?" Rachel asked, obviously not hearing my question.

"Yeah, that was me. You heard?"

"Sure did. You sound a lot different compared to real life," she said.

I wasn't sure whether that was a compliment or and insult. It didn't matter.

"Yeah, I guess I'll be doing weekends from now on. I'm stoked. So, why did you stop by?" I questioned again.

"You sure sounded great, my big Superstar DJ," Rachel purred.

Wow! This was truly a different kind of conversation than we usually had. I was taken aback by such flattery.

"I wanted to see if you could get June 3rd off," Rachel

continued. "It's a Saturday night. I'd like it if maybe…you'd be my date for the senior prom. It's a few weeks away so you should have plenty of time to request that evening off."

Following her invitation was a long, silent pause.

"Aaron?"

After burying my face in the pillow to keep her from hearing me scream excitement, I heard her call my name again.

"Yeah, yeah…ahem. I'm h…h…here," I stuttered. "Did you s…say something about wanting me to take you to the prom?"

So was I the last man on earth? Did the high school quarterback already have a date? Why me? Heck, I couldn't care less. Rachel Meyers had asked me out to the prom. I could finally die now. I'd seen and heard it all!

"Yo, Romeo, your boyfriend is here! Get off the phone!" yelled the boisterous Halo over my shoulder. "Call her back. We got business to discuss."

Halo threw himself onto the couch and tossed his legs up on the arms, flashing his sarcastic smile.

"I…I gotta go," I said into the phone.

"Go? Go where? To the prom with me? Great, Aaron!" Rachel cried. "We will catch up later to discuss the details. I'll chat with you soon!"

She hung up before I had a chance to thank her. This was great news, but I'd better not share it with the company around me so as to start trouble.

"Don't play me a fool, Dookie. I overheard the conversation in the other room. Prom, huh?" questioned Halo, raising an eyebrow.

"Yeah, it's no biggie. We're just friends," I said, playing it off modestly while I did cartwheels in my head.

Halo studied me through his yellow tinted Arnette sunglasses, as if trying to read my mind. Only Eddie could do that, and I could tell he already knew that something big had just happened. Before he had a chance to ask what went down, Halo interrupted, "Hmmmph, that's cool and all. It's just too bad she's a DJ ho and all."

"DJ ho?" Eddie gasped. "I don't know about that. She's always been really cool. It's not like she sleeps around or anything. What is this all about?"

Halo shrugged and leaned back, cupping his hands behind his head. "You obviously don't know Rachel the way I do, or *did* last night anyway, hee hee."

That remark sent shivers up my spine. Was it true? Did Rachel just want to show me off to her high school friends because I was an "on-air personality"? Judging by our recent conversation, I couldn't help but think that this guy could be right. And if Halo had been "with her," there was no way I'd ever want to be.

How slutty! She had just met this arrogant jerk a couple of days ago.

"So..." I interjected, trying to change the subject, "you want to throw a party, I hear?"

Halo swung his body around to let his feet touch the floor and started to wave his hands as he talked.

"Yeah, fer sures. I want to do one myself, this time, because the promoter from the last party walked away with a grip of cash and never came back. I'm gonna revive the rave scene, man! In fact, I'm gonna call my first party 'Revive.' Maybe make this an annual thing, ya know? But we will see how things go with the first one."

"Where are you gonna throw this at? Masonic Temple?" asked Eddie.

"Nope, we lost that joint due to some tweakers that went nuts at the last party. They busted into the office and sprayed the computers with a fire extinguisher." Halo stood up and started to pace. "I know of a place we can use for the night. It's so dope! Two levels. We can have the main room, and the basement can be our chill lounge. I checked it out the other day and it's got this cool room backstage that has a ladder you can climb to get to the light trussing. You can see the whole dance floor from up there. Only VIP will be able to get back there. Wicked, wicked stuff."

"This venue, it's legal, right?" I asked, fearing the worst. "I mean it's not like we are breaking into the place or anything, right?"

"Don't worry about it, Dook. It's all under control," Halo said suavely, a weird smirk on his face.

"So what do you need from me?" I asked. "You know I can't spin like you."

"Well, I could use you to promote this. You work for some radio station, right? I figured you can plug my party on the air," said Halo, staring down at me. "You can do that for me, can't you?"

"Yeah, I suppose," I said, without asking for anything in return. This would actually benefit me in the long run, I figured, as I could introduce myself to the people behind the scenes and further myself in my ambitious attempt to get ahead in the DJ industry. "No problem."

"That's great. I knew I could count on you, Dookster. Time to celebrate!"

Halo sat back down and reached in his coat pocket to pull out a Ziploc bag filled with yellowish powder. He shook it in front of Eddie's face, then dumped the contents on the coffee table and chopped it up with a library card. Eddie sat next to him and began to roll up the only dollar bill he had in his pocket.

I had heard stories about this stuff. Some called it crank, some meth or glass. There were so many street terms for it, it was hard to keep up on the latest lingo. Regardless, I wasn't going to touch it.

I stood up and headed to the bathroom to take a shower and get ready for work.

As I passed by Halo, he raised his hand and gave me a high five. "Right on, right on. Thanks for your help, big man. Make sure you have Saturday, June 3rd, off of work. That's when Revive is going down."

Chapter Nine

DJing the weekend overnight shift for The X had totally thrown off my sleeping schedule. It was difficult to get my pattern of rest back to normal after two shifts that required me to stay awake until eight o'clock each morning. By the time Wednesday rolled around I'd be back on track, waking around 9 AM. But when the weekend arrived it was all about the Mini-Thins to keep me up and alert.

When I rolled into bed in the morning, most of the western hemisphere was awake but me. But when I was on the air from midnight until the sun peeked out from behind the massive Spokane skyscrapers, those were the night hours when the freaks came out in droves. I didn't want to categorize myself as one of the freaks, yet it was truly difficult not to feel like one, especially when my job required me to interact with them. I concluded that the only people listening to my red-eye shift were janitors (who cleaned up after other people that were neatly tucked into their beds), bank robbers (who stayed up all night to make their break-ins while the city lights were dimmed), night owls (returning from after-hours parties), or insomniacs.

My favorite listeners were girls who called in half drunk to flirt with me. That kept things interesting. However, Johnny had warned me that these ladies were truly dogs. Ugly! So it was in my best interest to never arrange a meeting with one of them outside of work.

I learned this the hard way when a vampish female with a Sandra Bullock-like voice convinced me to rendezvous with her at the Northtown Mall one afternoon. I played it smart and arranged to meet her in the food court where there would be a bunch of people and I could easily observe her from afar without giving myself away. I told her to wait for me at the bench closest to Arby's, at 3:00 PM. Needless to say, she was no Sandra Bullock...more like Sandra Bernhard. Gap-toothed, Volkswagen-bumper lipped, cat litter complexioned...You get the idea. Yeah.

Still, this sort of girl kept me awake as one after another called in requests. What the listeners did not know, however, was that we never played requests! I mean, unless it was a "lunch-hour-all-request-show" or something that was billed as a request program, the DJs were instructed to never play a song out of rotation. We had to follow the hourly logs as if they were scripture. If a DJ were ever to deviate from that rule he was kicked to the curb by the program director. The only time we made an exception was if the hour was running short, which seldom occurred since Johnny crammed so much music into each hour that it was usually impossible to find extra time.

I had to come up with clever ways to get out of playing a song, without explaining why we couldn't play it. I'd say things like, "Yeah, I'll write it down," or, "Sure, I'll start looking for it." That usually sufficed. More often than not, the song they requested was going to come up in rotation, anyway.

I'd usually have to fight to keep from passing out from 3:00 AM until 6:00 AM, because that's when the phones would die down. During the really long songs, I would stand up from the control board to stretch and just roam the halls of the dark, five-story building. Often I'd cue up a song about four to five minutes in length, then run to prep the elevator so that it would be on my floor. I'd scurry back, push play, then return to the elevator so I could smoke a cigarette in the parking lot and be back in time to announce the next song.

I had never smoked until I started working there. One time in high school, a friend let me have a drag of his cigarette and I almost coughed a lung out. But when Johnny heard one of my audition tapes and criticized me for sounding like Peter Brady in puberty, he forced me to walk outside and instructed that I smoke three Camels in a row. He said it would deepen my shrill voice. I guess I believed him.

After that, cigarettes became quite satisfying and actually gave me an excuse to go outdoors once in a while for a "breath of fresh air." Plus, it seemed everyone who was anyone at the station smoked, so I was included in really interesting conversations around the ash tray with the "big boys."

I also learned quickly that in the radio industry you have to put in lots of volunteer, unpaid time to get anywhere. This means that if you want to make it far in this business you must sacrifice schoolwork and keggers to devote time to random tasks that the programming or promotions managers would rather not do. The hours vary widely from one week to the next. One weekend the station could be broadcasting live from a local car dealership; the next you could be sitting behind a mixing board, piping down live feeds from the arena for the hometown hockey game.

In order to stay ahead of the competition, you have to learn it all. If you want to be a music director of a radio station and have some say in the song rotation, you have to work many months, even years, to familiarize yourself with terminology and musical formulas. You have to gauge things like TSL (Time Spent Listening), the amount of time an average listener tunes in. Average TSL is only seven minutes in Spokane. Think about it! It takes only twenty minutes to make it from the valley to the north side in that town. If you are in your car, you have certain distractions that keep you from paying close attention to what is on your radio. The odds of your listening any longer than seven minutes will vary, especially if you are at work. However, the Arbitron (the Nielsen ratings-like system for gauging radio listenership) clearly states that most stations on the Spokane dial receive only that amount of listener dedication.

One of the music director's many jobs is trying to keep folks listening longer. One trick is to position the most familiar music inside a "sweep" (a long stretch of music) before each "stop set" (a long stretch of commercials). You would think it would be about the music, right? Wrong. The reason you are able to sing along to almost half the songs on the radio is that the industry bombards you with recognizable tunes to keep you roped into sticking through the commercials. This is how they make their money. If a music director is smart, he will follow a stop set with a "smash single," something almost everyone knows, so that his audience is compelled to hang in there.

There is little room to experiment. Newer songs are sandwiched between familiar ones, so they will be recognizable the next time you hear them, which will be in about an hour and an half. The biggest complaint radio insiders get is that the same songs are played in the same rotation over and over again until they are beat to death. Why do you think that is? Because every time you tune in, the station wants to hook you into its "captive audience" with the lure of recognizable hits.

I remember one time when I drove from downtown to Northtown Mall, listening to a new hit song. I was rolling into the parking lot and when I cut the engine the radio turned off half way into the chorus. When I arrived back at the car after about ninety minutes of shopping, I turned the key and the song was on the radio at the exact syllable where I had left it. It was as if I had stopped a CD when I switched off the ignition. Funny stuff.

While music directors perform their role, there are many other players who help create a winning team. A good sales staff, for instance, is equally essential. No clients, no money, no radio station; that's the way it works. Each day the sales crew leave their office cubicles around 9:00 AM, cell phones in hand, with lists of contacts. It's all about proving to small and big businesses that this is the perfect station for their customers. It's their job to convince businesses that listener demographics will relate to their product. For example, you wouldn't advertise a teenage dance club on a classic rock station. You'd want to put it on a Top 40 station.

There are companies that own more than one radio station. The sales staff must be able to customize packages that will offer potential customers proper placement on the proper stations. It sounds simple, but it isn't. There is no way I could do what these people do. For one thing, the competition is cutthroat and keeping in constant contact with clients to make them happy would be enough to make me explode.

Every day it's something new with the clients. Some nightclub wants a new spot run to promote their weekend show and they want it to run yesterday. A campus bookstore is calling to complain that they heard a head shop advertised right before their ad last night.

The money can be very good and I'm sure that's the motivation behind choosing this angle of the industry, but the turnover rate in sales staff is far more rapid than on the programming side.

Then you have production. These are the guys who sit around for hours slaving over dubs and feeds and jingles and scripts. All of this is done to create the commercials the clients order and the "positioning" for the station. Positioning is the stuff you hear in between the songs: "Today's lite rock" or "Better hits from today and yesterday," that sort of thing.

The tireless production staff sits in front of computer screens, editing machines, and reel-to-reels all day, every day, to make the station sound larger than life. Without them, all we'd have is music. (Personally, I would prefer it that way. Wouldn't we all?) Regardless, in order to justify the station's receiving any revenue from advertisers, they have to constantly remind listeners what station they are tuned in to. That way, when the Arbitron survey is handed out randomly, people mention the station because they've heard its slogans or call letters again and again.

For the promotions department, it's not exactly about the music or sales, but about the street presence of the station. If you are a hip radio station, you need to be where the coolest concerts are or inside the hottest nightclubs. If you are targeting an older clientele, you need to hook up with some swanky restaurants, foreign car dealerships and wine distributors, because listeners of that age support these types of services.

If you were interested in becoming an on-air talent, your best bet would be to start out as a promo tech and work your way up. This is the best position to acquire if you really want to get to know who your listeners are. A promo tech is the grunt boy, the one who sets up the station's tents, hangs banners and tears down after each event. He's never bored, that is for sure. And although the pay is dang near non-existent, the benefits (i.e. freebies) are plentiful. You get to go backstage, you always get free food and free CDs. Plus, the connections you make with the community and clients are priceless. It's only a matter of time before you are no longer ID'd anywhere you go. It's always VIP all the way.

Being a very determined individual, I was willing to do anything to get a leg up in the biz. So when Johnny offered me my first big task, I quickly jumped at the chance, not realizing what was in store for me at the time.

Chapter Ten

It had been a few weeks since I had spoken with Rachel. I felt kind of uncomfortable getting ahold of her lately, since Halo had shared with me their little escapade. Plus, with Revive on the same night as her prom, I was torn about what I should do that night.

I considered the rave to be a job shadow position. My goal was to be one of those turntable DJs like Halo, and if I were to miss out on that party I'd be holding myself back from doing what I really wanted to do with my life. I wasn't about to wait until Halo threw Revive Two to get in the game.

So I decided to be stubborn and wait for Rachel to call me again. If she really wanted me to go to her prom, she had to convince me that it was Aaron she wanted to go with, and not Dookie.

During the weekdays I would go out and help Halo promote his upcoming event. He had designed an awesome quarter page flyer to distribute, five-thousand or so. We'd start in the late afternoon every day, around the time kids were getting out of class, and just hang outside the main doors of the high schools, passing out flyers to anyone and everyone (except teachers and staff, of course).

Around five-ish was when we'd hit the mall or coffee shops and at the end of the day I'd put my fake ID to use and sneak into the bars with Halo. Nightclub security and club owners never took a liking to us promoting inside their establishments. They felt that it would take away from their client base. So, we had to keep it on the QT and be sneaky with our promotions in certain places.

One afternoon we decided we should make a billboard on an old rundown brick wall that faced Monroe Street downtown. It looked as if it was a support foundation for a bridge at one time, or perhaps a railroad. Many people before us had used it to paint marriage proposals or generate school spirit before rival ball games.

Halo and I had borrowed some paint supplies from his father's garage and we began to paint a huge mural similar to the design of the flyer. I took the top half and he took the bottom half.

It was starting to get dark and we were about through with the beautiful painting when a police car spotlight shone on the wall.

"You know that is considered vandalism, right?" barked the beefy officer who, stepping out of the car, resembled a brick wall himself. "I could have you behind bars for this. What is it you two are doing anyway? What is 'Revive'?" he questioned, taking out a notepad and cocking his head to view the freshly painted mural.

I froze in fear. I recognized this man as Officer Conrad, a friend of my family since he had been a neighbor when I was a little kid. His appearance tonight was not as a routine patrolman. He had worked his way up through the ranks of the SPD and was now Sergeant of the tactical force; you know...crowd control, that sort of thing. His chance observation of our prank had me sweating bullets. All I needed was for my mother to get wind of this!

Halo, on the other hand, was as cool as an Eskimo drinking a slurpee. "Relax, Dookie," he said, seeing my pale face. "I got this covered. Just stay here."

He casually hopped down off the wall's platform. "Evening, officer," he said with a smile. "I realize that this may look awfully fishy but I can assure you we are doing this for all of the right reasons."

"Oh, really," smirked Conrad. "Exactly how is vandalizing city property considered a good thing?"

"Sir, do you believe in Jesus Christ, our savior?" Halo asked, confidentially
placing his arm around the cop's shoulder.

My eyes must have been as big as LP turntables. What on earth was Halo up to? I knew Conrad was a religious man, as he had attended the same church as my mom and dad attended before their divorce. Was Halo mocking him?

"Why, yes, yes I do," Conrad said in bewilderment. "What on earth does my faith have to do with what you kids are painting?" he asked, as he tensely moved out from under Halo's fake affection.

"Well, I'm afraid you'll have to excuse my partner in crime up there," Halo replied smoothly. "What Aaron meant to spell was 'Revival,' not Revive. You can see how the two words are similar, can't you? I was just about to tell my brother in Christ to change the lettering, but not until after we were finished with the rest of the design so the paint could dry."

"Hmm. I see," Conrad said, rubbing his chin and looking quite leery. "And where, exactly, is this *revival* to be held?"

"It's being held at the...at the..." Halo paused for the first time, obviously struggling for an answer.

"It's being held at Riverfront Park," I said in a squeaky voice.

Conrad registered recognition as he looked at me. Could it be he remembered me from all those years ago?

I swallowed hard and hopped off the wall, amazed as my lying lips spun more deceit. "Inspiration Point on the north end of the park," I continued, gesturing in that direction. "All denominations are welcome to join us for an afternoon of rejoicing and worship. We will finish with a candlelight vigil and songs of praise as the sun sets."

"Inspiration Point, eh?" said the officer, placing his notepad back into his shirt pocket. "I go there often myself. Most every Sunday, after church. It's a very spiritual place. So did your church get a city permit to hold an outdoor event?"

Halo finally took an easier breath and proceeded with confidence.

"We sure did. Would you like to see it?" he replied. "It's in my car. I'll go get it!"

Halo started to walk up the hill toward the parking lot, as if to grab the papers. His back was turned toward the officer and he looked directly at me with huge eyes as if to say, "Help!"

"No, no. That's fine," Conrad said. "But, listen. I take my job very seriously and MY relationship with Christ even more so. If I find that you are just making all of this up to save your hide then you will suffer the consequences of your actions. Do you unders..."

The officer was cut short by Halo's interruption. "Yes. Yes, we do understand, officer. So, please be a saint and allow us to spread the word, much like His disciples, by finishing this labor of love."

Conrad's jaw clenched, and his eyes narrowed. "Very well, carry on," he said at last.

When he had trekked back to his patrol car, turned off the spotlight and gotten in, Halo flashed me a huge grin.

"Dookster, we make a great team! Excellent save, my friend. You sounded like a true Bible thumper there for a minute. Heck, you almost convinced *me*!"

My fists formed hard knots and my face burned with shame.

"Listen, man," I responded, "it's not like I wanted to get involved. I saw you were about to lose that guy's trust, so I had to chime in. You realize how bad I feel having to use the Lord as an alibi for our wrong doings? I just didn't want to see you or me get thrown in the slammer. And since you brought the whole Jesus thing up first, what was I supposed to do? Stand there and watch you fry?"

I could see that Halo was getting hot under the collar. "Whatever, man, I saved us," he spat. "That's all that matters, and it was all I could think of at such short notice. Analyze it however you want. If it weren't for my smart thinking, we could have been in the back of that car in handcuffs. I got us off the hook, so lay off, *Jesus freak*!"

I quickly gathered up the paint supplies and headed toward Halo's car. As I hit the sidewalk, the police car was just pulling away. Conrad's eyes met mine with a strangely sad look that went right to my gut. Had he overheard our conversation?

I was stunned. Wheeling about, I shouted at my fellow delinquent, "You may have saved us this time, Halo, but it's too bad that we're going to hell because of it! Can your smart thinking save us there, too?"

I threw the paint in the back of the car, jumped in the passenger seat and slammed the door, motioning to him to get on the road.

The drive home was a silent one.

Chapter Eleven

I soon realized that even though I had my foot in the door of the heritage Top 40 station I was still a far cry from being considered a "big boy" in the radio game. Weekend overnights were the least listened to timeslots, as Johnny had told me while socializing over the ashtray. He said it had taken him over two years to finally get the recognition he deserved in this company.

That seemed like an awfully long time to struggle with sporadic hours and minimal scheduling. Still, if I wanted to make it, I'd have to pay my dues, just like he and all the rest.

That was the least of my career troubles, however. The hardest part for me were the restrictions that were put on me when I announced. "It's all about the music and not about you," Johnny pounded into my head over and over again.

Perhaps, but what kind of fun was that? It was hypocritical for him to say such a thing, anyway. Every other word that came out of his mouth was his own name.

I allowed myself a certain amount of freedom during the times that I figured Johnny was asleep, usually around four in the morning.

It was when I let loose and started to be more myself that I had the most phone calls. Listeners went out of their way to contact me at that time and let me know that the things I said were the funniest they had ever heard on this station. Some were even bold enough to express that I should have replaced Johnny during his night show. I was really taken aback by these compliments, since I had been a DJ for only a few weeks.

It seemed that the "freaks" were able to identify with my witty observations. Maybe all these people wanted was a friend; night was an awfully lonely time for all of us.

We kept each other company and it was as if I was the guy who would come over to their houses, bring a whole bunch of CDs and just kick it with them.

Granted, I'd occasionally get caught by Johnny while "being

myself." He'd ring in on the hotline to keep me humble, or warn me with the "Bat Phone," a silently flashing red light above the mixing board.

Still, I could tell by his tone of voice, when he chewed me out, that he, too, enjoyed my banter.

****

Despite my professional strides, I was having a rough time getting by.

Living with Eddie was starting to get on my nerves. It was difficult to keep up with his party regimen. People would come over at the strangest times; maybe for only a few minutes, but occasionally for several days at a time. Sometimes he'd be up around the clock, just carrying on conversations with random tweakers, and his friends would get so annoying and loud that I'd have to sleep in my truck.

It was then that I began to frequent Inspiration Point.

A few weeks had passed since the ordeal with Halo and that cop. I felt guilty about the way things had gone down that evening and I figured I'd pay respect to the place I had used as a scapegoat to get us out of that potential altercation with the law.

Plus, I wanted to experience Inspiration Point sober; I had been coming off a synthetic high when I first discovered that "spiritual place." I figured it was only fair to return with a clean head and pray for forgiveness and for a brighter future.

One morning something happened that raised my hopes. A guy called in during my shift and drilled me with a whole Twenty Questions routine. I didn't get his name, but it seemed like he knew a lot about the industry. Perhaps he was an air personality who was just passing through, I thought.

He asked things like: "Where have you announced before?" "How well do you know this market?" and "Have you ever wanted your own talk show?"

I felt comfortable answering his questions because he seemed sincere and non-threatening. But when he was through with his interrogation, he just said "thanks" and hung up.

60

What was that about, I wondered. I figured perhaps it was a set up to see if I was loyal to the station, but I did indulge the fantasy that it was a recruiter of some sort. I thought, "Man, wouldn't it be great if some programmer from MTV was passing through town, looking for fresh talent?"

I have always had an active imagination. But, it was thoughts like that that kept me alert and awake during those rough overnight shifts.

Chapter Twelve

It was about eight o'clock in the morning. I was fading fast because the night before had been a rough one. Ed had had about half a dozen meth heads talking it up until the wee hours, so I hadn't slept very well. It was a struggle to keep myself from passing out, but I managed to survive through my final announcement.

I had just signed off when the hotline rang. I was tempted to ignore the call and let the next DJ deal with whatever Johnny wanted. However, a sense of responsibility got the better of me and I decided to answer the call.

"Dookie, we need you down here," the boss announced.

The X was preparing for their live broadcast for Hoop Fest, an annual three-on-three basketball tournament. Each year in our town, about fifteen square blocks are sectioned off to make room for some one-hundred makeshift half-court basketball arenas. It was the radio station's responsibility to cover the action by announcing over loud speakers that were placed throughout downtown. It was Johnny's team that had installed the speakers on overhanging street lamps the night before.

"I'm too tired to announce the play-by-plays this early in the morning. I need you to cover for me," Johnny instructed, sounding like he, too, was having a difficult time staying awake.

"I guess he doesn't know what it's like to live with a tweaker," I thought to myself.

"You are used to these hours I'm sure, so I'm going to need you for this. Get here right now, man," Johnny commanded.

By the time I reluctantly arrived downtown, the streets were filled shoulder-to-shoulder with ball-players warming up on the courts, and spectators who would soon root them on.

It took all the energy I had left to fight for a parking place on the crowded streets, so by the time I got to the announcer's booth I was ready to collapse on the concrete.

The booth stood high above the winner's court, the arena

where finalists would compete for this year's trophy and cash prizes. Inside the booth were a microphone, a CD player and mixing board, and a dozing Johnny, resting his head on the table.

"It's about time you made it," he groaned. He slowly rose from his seat and headed out.

"Wait!" I frantically yelled when he was half-way across the street. "What am I supposed to do?"

"Just announce the upcoming teams and what court they are playing on," he shouted back. "All the info is in front of you on that sheet of paper. Every now and then you may have to reunite a lost kid with his family and stuff like that. It's cake. You'll do fine." Johnny turned his back as if to leave again, froze in place and then spun around. "Oh, yeah, and you'll have to push play on the CD player to start The Star Spangled Banner at exactly 9:30. That kicks off the competition. Sheesh," he said, slapping his forehead, "I almost forgot about that! I must be totally out of it. I'm heading to bed. Dookster, make sure not to throw up on anybody this time."

It seemed like simple enough duties. And according to the schedule, someone from the station would be there to replace me at noon. Still, I was nodding off. Even the loud spectators and the bouncing of what sounded like a thousand basketballs couldn't keep me awake. I caught myself from falling out of my chair at least twice.

I rested my head on my hands and allowed my eyes to rest. My mind began to cancel out all the noise around me and I started to daydream.

Visions of the last rave I attended were bouncing in and out of my morning fantasy.

Lasers and intelligent lighting bounced from one side of my brain to the other. I pictured myself at Halo's vantage point, standing high above the crowd and tweaking the mixer from one record to the next. I'd raise my hands and the crowd would raise their glow sticks and Mickey Mouse gloves. I'd look behind me and see the crowd admiring my expert blending of one song into another.

From amidst the vast crowd a bright light emerged, floating from side to side of the dance floor. The light then approached the stage, ever so slowly, the dancers moving in slow motion as well. The luminous glow grew brighter the closer it came. Did I see wings? I swear I saw wings! Angel wings?

The light then drifted above the crowd. In the midst of the blinding radiance hovered a beautiful seraph, her arms raised above her. As she descended again, gliding gracefully toward me, I stepped away from the turntable and let my own feet leave the floor.

We embraced high above the dance floor while the sea of people swayed rhythmically below us.

Rachel! It was Rachel!

She softly pushed me away from her and held me by my shoulders. She gazed into my eyes and I got lost in hers. It seemed she was about to say something loving to me, but instead she began to viciously shake me. "Hey, hey you! Wake up! Wake up!" she yelled. I fell and I hit the ground hard. She laughed and disappeared.

Blinking away, I looked up to see a lady from the camera crew of a local television station standing over me. I had fallen because the chair had given way when she had shaken me.

I looked at my clock. It was 9:35!

"Sorry, guy!" laughed the woman. "You gotta start the opening ceremony with The Star Spangled Banner. Everybody is waiting on you. Hurry!"

I jumped to my feet, hustled to the CD player, pushed play and waited for the music to begin. Nothing happened. The timer on the display showed power, but no track number or countdown. I saw that a massive crowd was looking up into the announcement booth, expecting the opener.

I quickly pushed eject but there was no CD in the tray. I swiftly surveyed the booth to locate anything that looked like a crystal case or a disk. No luck.

"What do I do?" I asked the camerawoman, as she pointed her lens toward the impatient mob.

"I don't know, dude, but we are live so you better do something quick!"

Countless people were watching this broadcast. The people in the street began to mumble among themselves, obviously annoyed.

"Sing it!" whispered the camera lady.

"Sing it? Are you kidding? I barely know the..."

"Sing it!!!"

The camera was trained on me. The entire television audience could see the dark circles under my eyes and the absolute panic on my face. My helpless smile translated to two raised eyebrows and a jaw that dropped to my knees.

Realizing that my only hope was to abide by the suggestion. I grasped the microphone and began to address the audience. "Hey...so...howya doin', uh, everyone?"

Mutter, mutter.

"Um...welcome to Hoop Fest." I grabbed a sheet of notes off the desk, searching vainly for something relevant to discuss. "Jerry Hopkins, your child is waiting for you at the lost and found tent. Please report there immediately."

Grumble, gripe.

"Will you just sing the song?" the impatient camera lady uttered through clenched teeth.

I looked at the floor. *Johnny*, I thought, *if I ever get you I'll kill you!*

I took a deep breath, let it out and then inhaled once more.

"Oooooh say can you seeeeee, by the dawn's early light. What so proudly we hailed around midnight...at the twilight's last beam...gleaming. And the rockets' red glare! The bombs bursting in the...sky! Whose broad stripes and..." I paused to catch my breath. "C'mon everybody! Join in!"

Exasperated groans.

"Ahem. Gave proof in the night that our man was still there. Oh, say does that Star Spangled Baaanner yeeet waaaave. For the

laaand of the freeee...and the home of the brave!"
Gulp!
"Thank you! Play ball!"

Chapter Thirteen

It had been almost a month since I had heard from Rachel. I simply assumed that Halo and she were spending time together or that she had found a more suitable date for the prom, which was just a few days away. If she really wanted me to take her, she would have contacted me by now.

Buzz on the street for Halo's upcoming party was positive and enormous. Everyone I knew was going to be there or was making plans to show up after the Lewis and Clark High School prom. So even if Rachel were to call, nothing, not even the woman of my dreams, was going to stop me from attending this rave.

I awoke one #afternoon to the sound of the telephone ringing. Fearing that it was Johnny, I let the answering machine pick it up.

"Aaron, this is Rachel..."

I jumped off the hard floor and my stiff legs gathered the strength to carry me to the cordless receiver. I turned off the machine and cleared my throat. "Hey, I'm here."

"Where have you been? I've been trying to call you for over two weeks now. Didn't Eddie ever give you my messages?"

I looked to see Eddie on the couch with his feet hanging off one of the armrests and his head hanging upside down from one of the cushions. Drool waved back and forth from his mouth to the floor as he snored. I noticed that amidst the beer cans beyond the powdered coffee table were three other people, passed out on the floor beside him. People I'd never seen before.

I slapped my hand across his forehead. "Nooo, Eddie DIDN'T give me any of your messages, RACHEL!" He woke for only a second to utter some obscenity and then returned to snoring.

"Well, anyway," she sighed. "I wanted to let you know what time you can pick me up this Saturday."

"Um, yeah. About that. Halo needs me for his party. It's on the same night."

"You've GOT to be kidding me, right? This is a JOKE, right? C'mon, Aaron. Stop joking!" She was frantic.

I began to second-guess my decision, but then I considered what Halo had told me about their relationship. Besides, until I started to work at the station, Rachel had never shown any interest in me as more than a friend. I was convinced that she was just using me.

"Rachel, I can't. I just can't. I'm sorry. You can find another date, right?"

"In less than a week? Are you serious? Aaron! You FREAKING idiot!" Her voice was shrill with desperation.

"Listen, maybe you can....."

Rachel interrupted, "No! I'm not even about to have this conversation. This is the most important moment in a girl's life and you are telling me that some stupid rave is more important than this? I can't BELIEVE you!"

"Rachel, it's more complicated that that. Maybe you can come over and we can talk about thi..." I looked at my surroundings. "Maybe we can meet somewhere to talk about this."

"Forget it, Aaron!" She choked back tears. "Just forget I even asked!"

Before I had a chance to apologize, I was listening to a dial tone.

Eddie awoke just as I hung up the phone, "Yo, roomie. Rachel called for you last night."

"Thanks."

Chapter Fourteen

The time for Revive had arrived. I would have the stamina for this all night dance marathon because my midnight to 8:00 AM shift ended Saturday morning and I would have the chance to sleep right up to the point at which we were to set up. Johnny had given me Sunday off as well, so I was ready to party!

During my air shift I invited The X listeners to the rave. After each announcement, the phone lines lit up. It seemed everyone wanted more information about this techno gathering. Even those who called in song requests were subjected to my sales pitch about how this party would be unlike any other. Many were soon convinced that Revive was without a doubt THE event to attend.

Even The Shaman called in, inquiring about Revive. He didn't seem too happy, though. Saturdays were the busiest nights for his club. He asked where I had been lately and I explained that my shift kept me from coming out most weekends.

I asked if I could be his apprentice some Friday night, just to watch him do his thing so I could pick up some pointers on mixing. He agreed and gave me his contact info. We also made plans to meet on Wednesday.

My show went smoothly and soon afterward I was on the floor of Eddie's house, trying vainly to sleep. It's not that his acquaintances were keeping me awake. I had grown accustomed to the loud discussions and cracking open of cans and bottles. I was just too wired for the party.

I hoped that all of this anticipation had not gotten my hopes too high. Yet, it was hard not to be excited. We had put a lot of effort into promoting this event.   Eventually, though, I was able to control my breathing and rested well.

Around 8:30 PM, I arrived at the warehouse, a large brick building previously used for T-shirt manufacturing. I must have passed by it hundreds of times on my way to work. I'd never noticed it until Halo targeted it for his rave.

Paint chips littered the approach to the entrance door and deep gouges marred the frame near the busted door handle. It looked like someone had used a crowbar to pry it open.

The inside was just as Halo described, an enormous room with a loft, soaring ceilings and orange tinted windows. The basement was dark and gloomy, the perfect location for the ultimate, intimate chill room.

Halo's crew was busy setting up lights on the massive trussing high above the stage. The decorations committee was wiring camouflaged netting onto the ceiling rafters. They had already sprinkled glitter and tiny metallic stars all over the dance floor. I felt sorry for the people who would have to sweep up the next day.

The sound techs had already wired the sound system and one of the DJs had just finished performing a check on the wall of mammoth speakers when I walked in. It seemed everything was on point, but I was still concerned as to how Halo had "obtained" this building.

"Dookster! It's about time," Halo yelled as he approached me on the dance floor. Homeboy was decked out in ultra wide baggy jeans and wore a visor over his freshly tinted, glittered hair. "Listen," he said apologetically, "I'm really sorry I haven't spoken to you since we painted that wall. I've been super busy promoting and getting things in order. We're cool, right?"

Never the one to hold a grudge, I replied, "Yeah, it's all good. That's old news. What's really disturbing me is how..."

Halo interrupted, "We are all dialed in. Music begins in five minutes. Security is on point. Light show is programmed. Do this for me: roll up the road and grab us some smokes at the convenience store across the street. Here's some cash." He waved a ten dollar bill in front of my face. "Get a move on. You don't want to miss DJ Nitro's opening set."

It was too late for me to do or say anything. I said a feeble prayer for the safety of the partiers tonight as I walked briskly toward the mini mart.

A "DON'T WALK" sign at the intersection stopped me. While waiting to cross, I noticed a stretch limousine exit the freeway and pause at the red light.

Suddenly, I saw Rachel glaring at me from the passenger seat of the limo, her prom date by her side. As the light turned green and the long car sped off in the direction of the high school, my heart sank to my toes.

As if that weren't enough, a slow moving police car trailed the limo. As it crept past me, the cop also stared in my direction.

Officer Conrad? Don't tell me! I groaned to myself.

The dark silhouette of the law turned his head toward the old warehouse building and signaled his car in its direction.

Chapter Fifteen

Revive had begun.

I was just returning from the store when the first needle dropped onto the first record. Wild beats resonated from inside the building.

I did not see the cop car anywhere. I entered the warehouse and fought my way through the people waiting in the entrance to pay their admission.

As I approached the elevated stage, I saw Eddie standing too close to the wall of deafening speakers, fiddling with the police scanner's earpiece to get a better listen. "So far so good," he yelled up to Halo. "Most of them are on the north side responding to a meth bust. And there's one near our neighborhood for a domestic disturbance report."

So Conrad hadn't come here after all, I thought, breathing a sigh of relief.

"All right," yelled Halo. "Go tell Nitro to keep the volume down until the cop leaves the area, and keep me posted. If the police come in while I'm performing, grab Dookster. He's good at dealing with the po po's, aren't you, Dook?"

I pretended that it was too loud to hear what he was saying and made my way onto the dance floor. It was quite an ordeal getting through the crowd of frantic kids who were already swinging glow sticks to the rhythmic beat

About an hour into the event, it looked like there were nearly a thousand people there. By midnight the place would surely be over-capacitated.

I was amazed to see that so many had followed through with the task of calling into the voice mail line. I had figured that if anything were to keep them from coming it would be the fact that the mystery location was not revealed on the flyers, and they had to phone in to get it.

Of course, the police could have also called the line. Short of that, with Conrad driving by the jammed parking lot, it was a

72

wonder the whole SPD had not already been alerted. I feared it was only a matter of time before the police paid us a visit.

****

I made my way down the dark flight of stairs toward the chill room. The harder and faster tempo from the main floor faded into the floaty, hypnotizing rhythms pulsating from the basement. By the time I reached the bottom step and cleared the way for my large frame to fit through the hanging door beads, the music and atmosphere of the chill room took on their own identity.

This room offered a complete escape from the bedlam upstairs. Here one could relax and unwind. An inviting tray of fruits awaited the sweaty and exhausted dancers. Water flowed from a gurgling silver fountain and beanbags lined the fur-carpeted floor. The lowered volume from the basement speakers allowed the patrons to carry on conversations while sharing backrubs, or to sit in quiet corners, rolling joints.

The woodsy scent of patchouli and green bud began to permeate my clothing; all I had to do was sit there long enough if I wanted to get a serious contact high. It was for that reason that I opted to make my stay downstairs brief so that I'd be clear-headed, just in case my paranoia of authority became a reality.

****

I exited around the back of the basement and on up through the VIP hallway to enter the main floor backstage. Halo was behind the stage's backdrop, organizing records in his silver flight case, while DJ Nitro was finishing his last mix.

Next to the backstage entrance was a steep ladder that led up to the light trusses. I climbed the precarious steps to get a look over the musky curtains. Once I reached the top, I had an amazing view of the dance floor.

A sea of dancers swayed in an unorganized fashion below. Intelligent lighting cut through the crowd like a razor, creating swaths of blue, green, red and yellow. I tried to count how many people were there but lost track after fifty or so and had to keep starting over. It was clear that the fifteen-hundred maximum capacity was well exceeded by now.

But, suddenly, my interest in numbers was interrupted. Beyond the mass of bobbing heads, I saw her face!

Rachel stood out from the crowd because of her height and her formal attire. Her elegant black gown contrasted with the bright t-shirts and ponytails around her. She looked lost, but I knew what she was trying to find.

A short guy in a tuxedo rushed to keep up with her long strides as she made her way around the circumference of the dance floor. It seemed she was trying to lose him and she was succeeding. He finally gave up the chase and took a seat near the stage to wait for her.

I descended the ladder and parted the curtain. She was waiting for me as I stepped down from the stage. Halo was too busy to notice her as he cued up his first record. With one aggressive flick of the cross fader, his trademark air raid horn made the front row jump back and cheer. It almost knocked Rachel off her high heels, but I was there to save her from the fall.

I grasped her toned hips with both hands and she grabbed mine.

"You're here?" I marveled.

"Shut up," she yelled as she guided me toward the mass of people. "Just shut up, Aaron. I bought these shoes so that I could dance with you, not him." She looked toward her date and raised one eyebrow. Her vertically challenged companion was rubbing his neck and staring at the floor. Looking up at her all evening must have been quite painful for him. I can only imagine how the prom pictures had turned out.

Rachel placed my hands upon her slender waist and pulled me close. We wedged toward the center of the dance floor, and she wrapped her arms around my neck.

Everyone else danced solo. She didn't care. Neither did I. I didn't care about anything but that moment. This was the closest I had ever been to her, and despite the heat of the room, goose bumps rose all over me as her breath brushed my rosy red cheek.

The high-pitched tone of Halo's opening record soon gave way to a deep, resonating bass punctuated by a repetitive trance beat. Hypnotic rhythms led our bodies to sway in synchronized motion.

"Aren't they going to be jealous?" I asked, my lips close to her ear.

"They? You mean him?" she said as she nodded in the direction of her prom date. "I don't care."

"But what about Halo?"

"Halo? What are you talking about? You think he and I..."

I put my finger across her lips. I didn't need to hear any more. The moment was too perfect and we both knew it. Our feet stopped moving as I drew her soft lips close to my mine.

Her tongue lightly rolled across my half-opened mouth. As the beats became more intense, she fiercely drew my body snug against hers and let loose a deep sigh as we kissed.

I shuddered as my fingers rolled tenderly over her neck. She, too, quivered and had to move her head back every so often to catch her breath. Each time she did, I'd nuzzle my nose against her sweet smelling shoulders and I moved my lips up and down her long neck, exciting her more.

All through this set, we held each other in a hard embrace, not caring what kind of scene we were creating or who might be watching.

At last, Halo made way for DJ Marble. While the audience was cheering the DJs, I took Rachel by the hand and guided her up onto the stage. We passed right by Halo, who was too involved in his fanfare to notice, and we quickly ducked behind the curtains.

"Come here, I want to show you something," I whispered. She took off her heels and began to climb the ladder behind me.

"Oh my...look at how many people are down there!" she gasped, when we reached the high platform. "This is amazing!"

Rachel's legs draped over the top of the curtains and I knelt behind her. Below, in front of the stage, the chair in which her date had been sitting was empty.

"Well now, how are you getting home?" I asked with a grin.

"I have no plans on going home tonight," she said as she cuddled close.

She turned about and reached her hand toward my belt buckle. I started to shake all over. I had crazy visions of us falling off the platform right into the crowd below. But then, her teasing hand moved into my pocket. She grabbed my keys and pulled them out, a vampish smile on her face.

"I'll meet you at Eddie's house," she said.

I pulled back. "I'm not sure you want to go there. I can't guarantee that you'll be alone."

She swung her legs back toward the ladder and began to descend. "I'll take my chances," she laughed. "I'll also take your truck. See you there."

Chapter Sixteen

My neck and back were stiff from Eddie's hard floor, but lying next to her warm body all night must have calmed my nerves. I had slept like a baby.

I slowly raised my head to hear my vertebrae pop back into place and peeled one eyelid open to see what time it was on the wall clock. 2:30 in the afternoon. I pulled my sore self onto the couch and propped my head up to read the note Rachel had left behind. "I will call you," sandwiched between my name and hers, was all it said. While it was reassuring to know that she wasn't scared away by my snoring, the note was rather curt. A little too curt. No "thank you," no "last night was special," no nothing!

My head began to hurt. I decided I'd call her later that night. I wasn't about to take the chance of Ed forgetting to leave me a message if she contacted me.

I rested my cheek on the arm of the couch and surveyed the living room to find the elusive remote. I figured maybe the TV would distract me from jumping to conclusions, like I was so good at doing.

Suddenly, the screen door swung open, rattling against the side of the house. "No way!" yelled Eddie into the cordless telephone receiver, flicking his half finished cigarette onto the brown lawn. "Ah, snap!" He ran outside to stomp out the smoldering dead grass, then staggered back onto the porch, nearly tripping over the garbage that had accumulated on the lawn. "Listen! It ain't gonna be for too much longer...but he's...yeah...right....yeah...whatever. Bye."

"What was that all about?" I questioned. Then holding out my hand, "You got another smoke?"

I couldn't believe I'd gone through an entire pack last night!

Eddie fished through his baggy jeans. "They're spent. We gotta go get some more."

Sitting down next to me, he put his arm around me.

"Yo, bro," I grinned, pushing him away. "What's up with all

this affection? Feeling left out cuz you didn't get yours last night?"

I sifted through the ashtray and found the remnant of a cigarette.

"Light?" Eddie offered, flicking his Bic too close to my eyebrows. I snatched it from him and attempted to light it over and over without luck. Flick…Flick…Flick…

"Anyway, who was that on the phone?" Flick…spark! No flame. "Dang it!"

I stood up to look for a match. I could feel my entire skeleton pop and snap with each step. I paused to stretch my aching limbs.

"Dude, bro, buddy," Eddie replied, "you gotsta move out. I'm sorry. Landlord keeps drivin' by and sees your truck parked outside and thinks I got me a roomie."

"Well, you do, don't you? I *am* your roomie, right? Right? Roomie? Didn't you tell him you got a roommate?"

"Not exactly," he said, as he, too, dug for a used smoke. "I told him I had guests that come over a lot. But if your name's not on the lease, you can't stay here longer than three days. Sorry, man. It's his rules. I told him you'd be out by next week."

I went to the kitchen to light the butt by means of the oven. By the time I got back into the living room, the cigarette was completely inhaled.

"I'm gonna go get us a pack," I said. I zipped up my jeans, threw on my sneakers without tying them, and aimed for the door.

"What? Hey, hold up! Ain't we gonna talk about this?" Eddie pleaded.

"There really isn't all that much to talk about, is there, Ed?" I turned from the door to see him rising from the couch.

He spread his arms. "You aren't mad, are you?

He looked pathetic. All pouty and guilt stricken. I couldn't hate him. He had been gracious enough to let me stay here rent free for over a month.

I went to my friend and put an arm around his scrawny shoulders. "Ed, thank you," I said as I pulled away. "You did me a favor big time. I owe you."

"Yeah, but what are you gonna do?" Eddie asked, puffing his freshly lit butt.

"I'll manage. Don't worry. I've got some money saved up. I'll start looking for a furnished apartment. I have a paycheck waiting for me down at the station right now. It's enough for a first month's rent and that's about it. I'll have to skimp by for a bit, but I'll manage."

I tied my shoes and put on my baseball cap. "I'm out. Off to the station and to buy a pack of smokes. I'll get you one too, 'k?"

Eddie gave me a thumbs up as I walked out the door.

I actually did feel fine, considering. I didn't want to tell him at the time, but I was getting really fed up with his strange hours and the weird people who would bang down his door in the middle of the night. I suppose it really wasn't my place to say anything, since my name, after all, was not on the lease.

Also, I knew that if I were to stay there any longer I would start nagging him about his health. That would have started a huge fight. He had always been really defensive when it came to his choices and his life.

Still, I had noticed that he was rapidly losing weight and the dark circles under his eyes were becoming permanent. Surely his body was giving him the message to slow down, but he wasn't listening.

Yeah, I was actually glad to be moving on. Though I didn't know exactly where.

Chapter Seventeen

My neck and back were stiff from Eddie's hard floor, but lying next to her warm body all night must have calmed my nerves. I had slept like a baby.

I slowly raised my head to hear my vertebrae pop back into place and peeled one eyelid open to see what time it was on the wall clock. 2:30 in the afternoon. I pulled my sore self onto the couch and propped my head up to read the note Rachel had left behind. "I will call you," sandwiched between my name and hers, was all it said. While it was reassuring to know that she wasn't scared away by my snoring, the note was rather curt. A little too curt. No "thank you," no "last night was special," no nothing!

My head began to hurt. I decided I'd call her later that night. I wasn't about to take the chance of Ed forgetting to leave me a message if she contacted me.

I rested my cheek on the arm of the couch and surveyed the living room to find the elusive remote. I figured maybe the TV would distract me from jumping to conclusions, like I was so good at doing.

Suddenly, the screen door swung open, rattling against the side of the house. "No way!" yelled Eddie into the cordless telephone receiver, flicking his half finished cigarette onto the brown lawn. "Ah, snap!" He ran outside to stomp out the smoldering dead grass, then staggered back onto the porch, nearly tripping over the garbage that had accumulated on the lawn. "Listen! It ain't gonna be for too much longer...but he's...yeah...right....yeah...whatever. Bye."

"What was that all about?" I questioned. Then holding out my hand, "You got another smoke?"

I couldn't believe I'd gone through an entire pack last night!

Eddie fished through his baggy jeans. "They're spent. We gotta go get some more."

Sitting down next to me, he put his arm around me.

"Yo, bro," I grinned, pushing him away. "What's up with all

this affection? Feeling left out cuz you didn't get yours last night?"

I sifted through the ashtray and found the remnant of a cigarette.

"Light?" Eddie offered, flicking his Bic too close to my eyebrows. I snatched it from him and attempted to light it over and over without luck. Flick...Flick...Flick...

"Anyway, who was that on the phone?" Flick...spark! No flame. "Dang it!"

I stood up to look for a match. I could feel my entire skeleton pop and snap with each step. I paused to stretch my aching limbs.

"Dude, bro, buddy," Eddie replied, "you gotsta move out. I'm sorry. Landlord keeps drivin' by and sees your truck parked outside and thinks I got me a roomie."

"Well, you do, don't you? I *am* your roomie, right? Right? Roomie? Didn't you tell him you got a roommate?"

"Not exactly," he said, as he, too, dug for a used smoke. "I told him I had guests that come over a lot. But if your name's not on the lease, you can't stay here longer than three days. Sorry, man. It's his rules. I told him you'd be out by next week."

I went to the kitchen to light the butt by means of the oven. By the time I got back into the living room, the cigarette was completely inhaled.

"I'm gonna go get us a pack," I said. I zipped up my jeans, threw on my sneakers without tying them, and aimed for the door.

"What? Hey, hold up! Ain't we gonna talk about this?" Eddie pleaded.

"There really isn't all that much to talk about, is there, Ed?" I turned from the door to see him rising from the couch.

He spread his arms. "You aren't mad, are you?

He looked pathetic. All pouty and guilt stricken. I couldn't hate him. He had been gracious enough to let me stay here rent free for over a month.

I went to my friend and put an arm around his scrawny shoulders. "Ed, thank you," I said as I pulled away. "You did me a favor big time. I owe you."

"Yeah, but what are you gonna do?" Eddie asked, puffing his freshly lit butt.

"I'll manage. Don't worry. I've got some money saved up. I'll start looking for a furnished apartment. I have a paycheck waiting for me down at the station right now. It's enough for a first month's rent and that's about it. I'll have to skimp by for a bit, but I'll manage."

I tied my shoes and put on my baseball cap. "I'm out. Off to the station and to buy a pack of smokes. I'll get you one too, 'k?"

Eddie gave me a thumbs up as I walked out the door.

I actually did feel fine, considering. I didn't want to tell him at the time, but I was getting really fed up with his strange hours and the weird people who would bang down his door in the middle of the night. I suppose it really wasn't my place to say anything, since my name, after all, was not on the lease.

Also, I knew that if I were to stay there any longer I would start nagging him about his health. That would have started a huge fight. He had always been really defensive when it came to his choices and his life.

Still, I had noticed that he was rapidly losing weight and the dark circles under his eyes were becoming permanent. Surely his body was giving him the message to slow down, but he wasn't listening.

Yeah, I was actually glad to be moving on. Though I didn't know exactly where.

Chapter Eighteen

My new apartment rocked!

It was small, yet it had everything a single man could possibly need. Furnished with a bed, free cable TV, love seat, stove, end tables and more. I was stylin'!

Plus, it was in one of the coolest neighborhoods in Spokane: Browne's Addition, a quirky district with rustic mansions that had been redesigned to accommodate multiple renters. Each block had a cool coffee shop or antique store, and a 7-11 was right around the corner!

My building had the coolest neighbors, all around my age except for one older dude with a mullet that kept blaring Van Halen each morning at 6:30 through the paper-thin walls. I'd bang on the wall to get his attention, but he ignored me. I prayed that he didn't wake that early on the weekends.

It was Wednesday, three days after my world had been turned upside down. I kept picking up the phone every fifteen minutes to see if my new service had been turned on. That was my only link to the outside world and I grew impatient waiting. I had promised The Shaman last week that I'd call him to hook up, and I also needed to call around to find a new job. There was no point in going out to look for new employment if I didn't have a phone so prospective employers could call for an interview.

I started to go through my laundry, sorting out the dirty from the clean by means of the always-accurate sniff test. Eddie's washer never worked, so I often had to recycle my underwear by turning it inside out.

As I was filing the clothes into a plastic bag to take them downstairs to the communal laundry room, the phone number for the mysterious "Randy" fell out of last Sunday's jeans.

I sat down next to the phone and prayed once more for a dial tone. This time, I was in luck. Free at last! Free at last!

I dialed The Shaman first, and made plans to meet at his club later that day. I then broke out the black book and dialed everyone

I knew, to update them with my new contact info.

It took me about three hours before I finally decided to call this Randy guy back. Fearing the worst, I began rehearsing a list of excuses as to why his company had not received my payment.

"Gold Star Broadcasting, KHIT/KNGV," some woman announced, catching me completely off guard. "Can I help you?"

"This is a radio station?"

"Yes, sir. How may I direct your call?"

My heart beat fast and I stood up to nervously pace around.

"Uh, yeah…um…extension 45."

"And may I ask who's calling?"

"Aaron…Aaron Traylor."

"One moment."

There was a click and then the sound of music while I was on hold. It sounded like that alternative station I'd heard a few times before, located in Couer d'Alene, about thirty minutes east of Spokane.

Giveitawaygiveitawaygiveitawaynow…

Justgiveitawaygiveitawaygiveitawaynow…

After a few seconds, another click.

"Aaron? I'm sorry. Randy is busy at the moment. Would you like to leave a message?"

"Yeah, just go ahead and let him know Dookie from The X is calling and…"

"Dookie? Oh! Wait! Hang on!"

Click, more music.

What I've got you've got to give it to your mamma,

What I've got you've got to give it to your pappa,

What I've got you've got to give it to your daughter,

You do a little dance and then you drink a little water.

Seconds later, click again. "Dookie! You finally called! What is shakin', my friend?"

I recognized that voice! It was the dude who was drilling me with the Twenty Questions a few weeks back when I was on the air!

"Oh, wow! Hey you! What is up?" I instantly switched my voice into announcer mode.

"Dookie, we need to get together. I got something I think you might like to check out. How soon can you make it out to Couer d'Alene?"

I looked at the clock. "Give me an hour. I need to freshen up."

"Looking forward to it. I'll put you on the line with our secretary, who'll give you directions to the studio."

Once I got off the phone I jumped so high I hit my head on the low ceiling, creating a dent in the plaster. There went my damage deposit.

Nevertheless, I danced and screamed while rounding up my infamous polyester suit, the only clean article of clothing in my pile.

Giveitawaygiveitawaygiveitawaynow!!

Justgiveitawaygiveitawaygiveitawaynow!!

Mullet man next door pounded on the wall. I ignored him.

****

"We are changing format in a week. Latte'?" Randy offered, as he led me to a little coffee hut near the beach of Couer d'Alene Lake.

We strolled along the pier, soaking in the sun, and sipped our coffee as we got to know one another. This was unlike any other interview, informal and outside the confines of the office. I instantly felt comfortable with Randy.

"Really? To what?" I asked.

"Top 40. We plan to go head-to-head against The X." Randy stopped in his tracks to admire a pair of bikinied bombshells on roller blades passing by. "That's why I love working over here, you know. You get to see all of this from the window in the studio. It's great. Summers in Couer d'Alene are the best."

I couldn't disagree as I winked at his observation.

"How do you plan to beat The X?" I asked. "They are a powerhouse and they've been established in this market for as long as I remember."

"With you, of course. And with a little artistic freedom for all of our DJs. I'm looking for someone who is going to push the envelope." He continued walking.

"When you say things like 'artistic freedom' and 'push the envelope,' you mean...?"

"I mean a night guy with personality, someone who knows the music inside and out and is willing to actually communicate with his audience. Not just be a talking head who pulls his punches. You dig?"

"Night guy?" I nearly choked on my coffee. "You're serious."

"Johnny is getting old and he's always been cocky. When you start to get cocky, listeners can tell and it affects ratings. But there's a fine line between confidence and cockiness. You are confident; that is what I'm looking for. Dookie, I truly believe you've got what it takes to knock Johnny off his pedestal. There's something different about you."

Where had I heard that before?

I stopped walking and waited for him to notice that I was no longer keeping up with him.

He turned and smiled. "He fears you. You know that as well as I do. Listen..." Tony walked back toward me to put his hands on my shoulders. "I'm giving you a shot at the big leagues here, partner. I know you know what the kids want. You'll have complete control of your night show, you choose the music that's played, you decide the specialty shows, and I'll be the one that fine-tunes the whole package. No other night guy on the air has that much freedom, not even Johnny. You'll never have an opportunity like this offered to you again, because positions like this do not exist in the radio industry. Are you in? If you don't want it, I know of thousands of others who would die to have this chance."

Without hesitation I placed my hands on his shoulder as well. "Say no more, boss. I'm your man!"

Chapter Nineteen

"A mix show? You are kidding!" The Shaman was dumbfounded. "Man, and I thought we were just going to go out and cruise for chicks tonight."

We sat in the middle of the dance floor of Club Jungle, watching colorful beams of lighting bounce off the wall mirrors and disco ball. I had arrived earlier but we got too wrapped up in conversation to "cruise."

Since Randy had offered me this so-called artistic freedom, I wasn't going to delay on getting the ball rolling. I had been in Seattle a number of times and had heard turntable DJs mixing alongside of announcers over the airwaves. It sounded awesome and that was something I definitely wanted for my night show. I chose The Shaman over Halo as my mixer because I thought it was a more suitable fit. Shaman played remixes of the familiar Top 40 stuff, while Halo preferred the more underground style. Plus, Shaman wasn't a jerk.

All you have to do is plug your decks and mixer into the back of the control board and you'll be golden. I'll arrange for your own studio monitors and try to get you hooked up with some record labels for free product in return for your services." I smirked while putting my hands behind my head and leaning back. "You know, I'm giving you a shot at the big leagues here, partner. Are you in? If you don't want it, I know of thousands of others who would die to have this chance."

I laughed under my breath.

"So let me get this straight. You want me to do the mixing, you do the talking, and I get free music from the labels?" he pondered, rubbing his chin and raising an eyebrow.

"Nothing like this has ever been done before, not in this town. You are going to be the most well known mixer in Spokane." I flashed a big grin.

"Will I get to advertise my club?"

The grin turned to a serious stare. "Sorry, sport. Unless you got the money for the advertising you can't say a thing about Club Jungle, at all."

"You sure about that?" he asked.

"Trust me." I replied sternly, "I'm speaking from experience here."

"Let me think about this, OK?" Shaman stood up and started to walk toward the club exit. Then, he spun around quickly. "You got yourself a DJ!" He smiled and walked back toward me to give me a high five.

I jumped up and slapped his hand. "Excellent! Now...speaking of experience...I'd like to get some lessons from you. I really want to learn how to do what you do."

"What. Now?" he asked.

"Why not? The chicks can wait."

He shrugged. "Yeah, why not?"

The Shaman beckoned as he headed for the DJ booth. "Grab those headphones and splitter from the shelf."

He plugged his headphones and mine into the splitter, then jacked them both into the mixer between the two turntables. "I'll give you the basics tonight. Then you can watch me mix each time we are in the studio together. You'll soon catch on."

He fished through the crate of records behind the turntables, then paused for a brief moment and turned toward me.

"There is one major rule that each DJ has to follow while mixing for a nightclub or rave. You ready?"

"Sure thing!" I agreed, as I put my headphones over my ears.

The Shaman pulled one of the cans away from my head and whispered, "Look up." Then he snapped it back down onto my head playfully.

I pulled them down around my neck and asked what he meant.

"It's one thing to be in the zone. Mixing your hiney off. Your blending of music can be precise and on point, but if you are not reading the crowd you'll never be able to pull off a well-rounded performance. You can be the world's best beat matcher, but if you are not playing what the crowd wants to hear, you've lost. Look up. Observe their body movements. If they are getting burnt out, dragging their feet and breathing hard, it's time to switch it down before they walk off the dance floor. If you lose the floor completely, change. Change the pace, move from house to hip-hop or hip-hop to trance. Never classify yourself as one type of DJ or you'll only get one type of gig all the time. If you want to DJ at a club like this, you must be versatile. Know what they want before they know they want it and they will want to come back for more, week after week. Are you hearing me? Look UP!"

"Gotcha," I said, admiring the shiny sliders and volume controls on the mixer. "So what does this button do?"

"One thing at a time, Dookman, one thing at a time." He put his headphones down on the turntable and walked away.

"Hey! Is that it? I thought you were gonna teach me a few things tonight." I ran after him, almost choking myself with my headphones.

The Shaman cut the breaker and the intelligent lighting quickly dimmed.

"If you were listening, then you learned the most valuable lesson of all."

Chapter Twenty

"It's the new 95.9 KHIT, Spokane and Coeur d'Alene's hit music station! WHAT UP??? It's your night guy, Dookie. Here I am in front of a microphone again; this is where trouble usually starts. You know, with the prom season here once again it got me to thinking. Remember how your principal would always choose the band for the prom? You haven't truly enjoyed music until you've heard Boyz II Men on the clarinet. Get your requests in now before I make like a prom dress and take off. Here are the boys right now with 'I'll Make Love to You.' Yeah, right. I wish my girlfriend's parents didn't have a say in that matter. 95.9 KHIT."

Sure, it was corny. I know. But that's what the listeners loved. Stupid humor. The boss loved it, too. I'd get calls on the hotline each and every night with Randy splitting his sides on the other end. I just kept coming with them. What made me different from the rest was that I was not a "talking head"; I actually invited people into my personal life. My problems were theirs, and since I was around the age of my listening audience, they could easily identify with me. Most of them seemed to have gone through the same struggles with relationships as I had, or shared the same views when I expressed my opinions about life, music, even weather.

"95.9 KHIT, Spokane and Coeur d'Alene's new hit music station! Time to stick my finger out the window and get you an accurate weather forecast, this time brought to you by, brought to you by...me, I guess. We have no sponsor this hour. You may want to consider finding shade tomorrow afternoon if it's going to be anything like it was this afternoon. I swear I was on the beach earlier and I saw some dude DRINKING his potato salad. High of 95 tomorrow. Low of 65 tonight. Enjoy the cool temperatures while they last. I know I will because the boss here is too cheap to fix the cooling system in the studio. Yo! Don't get on me because I'm whining here. I don't need you calling in telling me about the pioneers making it without air conditioning! All those pioneers -- they're dead, you know. That's what people did back before air conditioning -- they just died."

What was most amazing was the fact that this five-nighttime-hours of utter idiocy was the most important thing I did all day. The hardest part about being a full-time announcer is meeting high professional broadcast standards. Yet, every evening, I acted as if standards didn't matter, like I just didn't care!

Fact was, this made my show popular. And it took hard work, though it couldn't come off that way.

I had a blast doing what I was doing and the phones lit up non-stop when I signed on each evening. It didn't take very long before I had a steady fan base. Unlike the rest of the jocks up and down the dial, I chose to actually play people's requests. In the small town of Coeur d'Alene, people appreciated that.

In fact, they actually sat outside the studio in the parking lot, cranked up their car speakers, and provided a small-scale party almost every night. I'd step out for a smoke every once in a while and people would swarm me, asking for autographs and free stuff.

****

"They really seem to like you, Dookie. Everyone is talking about the station and the new night guy," said Norm as he peeked his head over the mixing board counter. Norm was one of the unfortunates who were working their way up the ladder like I had at The X. Only he had it much worse. He'd sacrificed his social life to work overnights five days a week on the AM station next to my studio. He'd been working that shift for five years and never once had a chance to speak live on the air.

He was the guy who ran the Art Bell syndicated program, a strange and downright creepy talk show that focused heavily on the paranormal and supernatural. It must have messed with Norm's head. Night after night, he just sat around waiting to fire off the commercial sets until the show was through at 6:00 in the morning.

Norm was one of those bottle-lensed, thick-framed, four-eyed computer geeks who was better off awake when others were asleep. Yet, while everyone else seemed to ignore him, I actually took time to talk to him. I could tell he was really happy to have someone listen from time to time. Even though we spent only an hour together each day, I knew that it made his sorry life brighter just to have someone with whom to carry on a conversation.

"Yeah, it seems like it," I replied. "Wow, would you look at that? Man, you just don't see that everyday, do you?" Norm and I both laughed as a busty girl pressed her chest against the window with her shirt up around her neck.

"Do you suppose that was for me or you?" Norm asked, squinting his buggy eyes to keep his heavy frames from sliding off his oily nose.

"Are you kidding? She was looking at you the whole time, Norm. It's all for you, baby!"

Norm turned red, hit me in the shoulder and laughed. When he laughed he spit, so I had to cover my face.

I wished I'd had someone like me around when I was in junior high. I was the Norm of my school and I'd had few friends to talk or laugh with. Often I hoped that one of those jocks from wrestling try-outs would call in. I had conjured up many mischievous, vindictive plans over the years, and with the power of this radio station I could have made their lives even more hellacious than they'd made mine. Someday, I thought, my time of vengeance would come. I didn't know when, but I sure knew why, and I was ready to strike at a moment's notice!

"You're all jacked in, man! We ready to rock this town, or what?" I asked The Shaman as he practiced scratching in his headphones.

"You know it, baby!" he responded. "Let's get this party started!"

"All right then, quiet on the set. We's about to go live in three, two..." I pushed both mikes on.

"95.9 KHIT Spokane and Coeur d'Alene's new hit music station. It's Dookie and right behind me is my man! Getting ready to throw down like you've never heard before. All the music you hear at the clubs, we're about to bring it to you live from the studio right here, right now, for two hours. Sound check! Shaman, give me a scratch one time, show the people in the parking lot and the ones cruising the beach or on Riverside in downtown Spokompton how we do our thang!"

I raised the mixer slider up to full volume and gave them a swift dose of turntablism. The party people in the parking lot pressed closer to the window to get a better look. I could see one guy run back to his truck to crank his speakers up even louder than before.

"Yeah, that's right. Mike check one, two. Mike is on. Music on. This will put your system to the test. Shaman, drop the beat!"

The scratching quickly transformed into a glorious thumping Hip-Hop beat under my voice. I felt chills run through my body, because never before had there been this kind of music on the Spokane airwaves. Shaman and me? We were pioneers of a new sound for our area and the adrenaline rush kicked in full force.

"All right, I'm just going to let the beats ride for you and let my boy on the ones and twos bring it to you for two full hours. Non-stop, commercial free. It's the KHIT Hit Mix on 95.9 KHIT. Bring it, Shaman, bring it!"

I shut off the mike and stood up, but not before cranking the studio monitors up to full blast. I dimmed the lights in the booth and jumped up and down to the beat. The people outside jumped in sync with me. I raised my hands to cheer and the crowd outside went nuts.

When I could no longer stand the window of separation between our fans and me, I ordered Norm to open the doors and let a handful in. Before we knew it, the studio was shoulder to shoulder with ballistic teenagers.

The request lines were a constant stream of flashing lights. Everyone wanted to get through, because they wanted to be part of this moment.

The KHIT Hit Mix was about to go down in the annals of Inland Northwest radio.

Chapter Twenty-One

In my wallet was an office memo from Randy, which I carried like a portable trophy. It read:

"Dookums,

FYI:

KHIT 18-34 Females 7p-Mid=9 share,

KXXQ 18-34 Females 7p-Mid=10 share,

Welcome to the big leagues, partner.

Randy"

This meant I had the second largest night show in Spokane, coming in just behind KXXQ (The X) in market share of female audience between 7 PM and midnight. It had taken me only two rating periods, about seven months, to achieve that status.

I was breathing down Johnny's neck and The X was starting to feel the pressure!

In retaliation, Johnny had scheduled a mix show to go directly against ours. The difference was that it was syndicated, meaning that it came on CD pre-mixed with available talk time for him to make it seem as if it were live. It sounded good, from what I could tell, but I was on at the same time as he, so I never had much chance to really critique it.

If we were going to dominate the airwaves, then it was time to pull out the big guns, Randy thought. That was why I was called in to a roundtable meeting with the boss, The Shaman and the rest of the KHIT jocks.

"All right, thanks for showing up on time, everybody," Randy began. " Let's get this party started, shall we?" He pulled out a frosty case of draft and dropped it in the middle of the table. Every time a new ratings book came out, if we were moving up in the charts, we'd celebrate by cracking open a few cold ones. Everyone, including myself, tore into the half rack like a pack of thirsty hyenas, grabbing two or three cans at a time. I wasn't twenty-one yet, but the boss didn't seem to recall that.

"That's right, get loose, unwind. Relax a bit. Then we will get to the point of this meeting," said Randy, as he chugged his brew like a frat boy.

We sat back and shared a few laughs. There was nothing like jawing with a bunch of air personalities. Everyone had something to say and we were always trying to outdo each other with our witty remarks.

These people had become my friends. I had lost track of practically everyone I used to hang out with, because my shift conflicted with their party schedules. I mostly hung out with The Shaman, who'd crash at my house from time to time, because it was too far for him to drive home after our nighttime shift.

Still, a day didn't go by when I didn't think about Rachel, or Eddie. I promised myself I'd call Ed later, although I was afraid to see how he was holding up. The last time we had spoken was when I rounded up my belongings and moved out of his house. I was sure he hadn't slowed down much with his meth use and maybe it was best that I stayed away. Regardless, I was going to check in with him soon.

The beer was quickly polished off and we all began putting our heads together to see what could make our station better than the competition's. Everybody chimed in with bits of advice for each air shift and Randy took notes and tweaked the ideas. The morning show suggested an interactive trivia game and entertainment news column. The mid-day jock came up with the idea of broadcasting live each day from a sponsoring restaurant that could offer free lunch to random winners. Our afternoon jock came up with her own retro request program.

Finally, I was able to present an idea that had been rolling around in my head for far too long. "A talk show," I blurted out.

Randy was quick to point out that our AM station was for talk.

"I know, but this show would be a little different. Something that has never been done before," I said.

Everyone looked my way.

"If there is one thing I hate with a passion, it's dedication shows," I said. "Every radio station in town has its own version of them. All those sappy people calling in, talking about love this, and marry that. Blah, blah, puke. It's boring, it's been beaten to death and there is no way that everyone can be lovey dovey twenty-four hours a day, seven days a week. What if you've just had a bad day? Everyone has 'em! Bill collectors harping at you, getting evicted from your house, getting fired from your job or breaking up with your significant other. You know?"

They all nodded, and Shaman teased, "You aren't speaking from experience, are you?"

Everyone laughed, but I could tell they were wondering where I was going with this.

"I can't exactly say all that has happened to me in the span of one day," Randy laughed, as he put his pen down on the table and began to pay closer attention. "But keep going."

"OK." I stood up and paced the room. "Do you ever wish that there was someone you could call when your entire world is crumbling down around you? Everything seems hopeless and you'd rather not call your parents for their wisdom. Or perhaps your friends may not be answering their phones because they are tired of hearing you whine and complain. Maybe you want to get advice from someone who will listen but who won't care who you are or even what your name is."

"My husband is cheating on me and *hiccup* I have a rash under my armpits!" shouted Cindy, the afternoon announcer, shooting up out of her chair with her beer can held high. She was obviously a bit tipsy. I pulled her beer away and sat her back down.

"That's good. Good! A little too much information for us right now, but you are starting to catch my drift. This is what I say to you...Flush it! Get it out of your system! Start fresh and begin a new day, or life for that matter! Essentially, we will invite everyone to call in and complain and just get whatever ails them off their chests for good, be it anonymously or whatever. It not only will be therapeutic for them, but the people listening will get a kick out of it! They'll be like flies on the wall. Voyeurs without binoculars! All they have to do is turn on their radios! I will offer this service to my listeners and we will literally flush their troubles down the drain, and then give them a song request. One that will be appropriate for their situation. That's what I will do each night during the last hour of my show. I will call it… 'The Royal Flush'!"

"The Royal Flush," Randy repeated as he picked up his pen and began writing again. "Wow."

The DJs nodded their heads in complete agreement.

"And Cindy, as for that rash. Try switching deodorant. Just a thought."

"I think…I need to flush…something right NOW!" she burped, pushing me out of her way and making a bee line for the ladies' room.

Randy addressed the remaining staff members. "Well, let's call it good. Great work, team. I'll be speaking with you all individually about your show ideas tomorrow. You can go. Keep up the excellent work and have a good show."

Everybody filed toward the door, high fiving me on the way out. "You rule, Dookster. I'll see you later tonight," whispered The Shaman as he departed.

Before I could leave, Randy called me back. "Dookie, could you shut the door for a moment?" He motioned for me to sit down again.

"Listen, if it's about that dead raccoon in the studio, it wasn't mine. Blame the morning show," I grinned.

Randy laughed, and then continued, "As you know, the Coeur d'Alene Christmas parade is next week and the city has invited us to be a part of it this year. This is quite an honor and I'm hoping I can trust you with handling it, because everyone wants to spend Christmas Eve with their families. You and Norm would be the only ones available for the parade that night. Now, Dookie, this will be your first time out in public representing a radio station since that whole Hoop Fest fiasco, so I'm hoping that you will do better this time around. Just don't sing and everything should be fine. All I want you to do is drive the station vehicle and wave. The Shaman can join you if he wants. Cool?"

"Cool. You can count on us, boss," I said as I crossed my legs and put them on top of the round table.

"Excellent. I knew I could count on you. Now, I've also been doing some thinking...What if our radio station were to put on a party of gigantic proportions?"

I threw my feet to the floor and leaned forward. "Party? What kind of party?"

"Well, I heard about that Revive event you helped throw and I was wondering if our listeners might support something of that nature. You know, a rage. Isn't that what you call them?"

I giggled. "Um, no, boss. They're called raves and you know I'd be happy to help! I've thought about throwing one of my own, but I never had the money..."

"Until now," Randy interrupted. "In January our new budget will arrive, allowing me a little extra cash to play with. I'm a gambling man and I feel that you have the ability to..."

I stammered, running over my own words: "To double, triple, even quadruple your investment! I could talk it up during my show! We can produce full color flyers with our station's logo, enough for Spokane and Coeur d'Alene! The Shaman can headline! He could rent out his gear and shut down his club for the night so there wouldn't be any competition. Ah, man! It would be outrageous. Oooh! Oooh! I could open!"

Randy tried to keep up with my rambling, taking down as many notes as he could. "Wait, slow down. Open? You mean perform? I didn't know you could spin."

"Well, I'm not The Shaman, but I've been practicing and by the time the party happens I'll be good enough to play for an hour at least. Please? Please?" I cupped my hands together and shook them in front of Randy.

He looked up from his pad and smiled. "If you say so. So you think you can make this happen? I'm counting on you once again to give our radio station the edge over The X. We need to give the impression that we are hip and street wise if we want to win the battle."

I'll start looking for a venue tomorrow and I'll talk to The Shaman about this tonight!"

I leaped out of my seat and skipped toward the door.

"Oh, yes. About that. The venue…it needs to be legal. Not some rusty warehouse where people can get hurt. Proper fire exits, handicap entrances, insured. I know that's not what you had for Revive. Our station can't afford to get sued, Dookie."

My first thought was that I'd lose the core rave audience. People who went to these parties wanted a sense of danger when they arrived. They wanted the feeling that they were doing something naughty, even borderline illegal. I thought, "Who would want to go to a rave at some hotel banquet hall?"

Then I realized that if I looked hard enough I could find a place that would suit everyone's needs. It would just have to have the right kind of atmosphere. Dark, dirty, and industrial…only legal.

"I'm on it, Randy. Thanks. Thank you so much!"

Chapter Twenty-Two

"Randy has got to be kidding! There's no way we will ever get noticed."

Shaman and I stood in one of Coeur d'Alene's dark alleys in awe, looking at the massive 4H Club float with its exquisitely decorated Christmas tree. It looked like it touched the sky. The Coeur d'Alene High School drill team practiced their tambourine twirling and amazing aerial flips behind us. And here we were, standing next to a Mazda mini van with station logos slapped on the hood and side panels.

"I can't believe this is all we have to show for our station," I griped. "Three guys in Santa hats and a family van. This is stupid!"

Norm peeked his head out the window of the heated vehicle. "Hey, guys, I think I see the floats ahead of us starting to move! Get in!"

"Shaman, can you believe this? Why are we even here?" Steam rose from my mouth into the frigid air when I spoke. "Randy said the new budget doesn't kick in 'til January. That would explain the lack of decorations. I just hope he's got enough to pay us for this."

"Come on," Shaman said with a shrug. "Let's just get this over with. I'm freezing."

I had to think fast. I wasn't about to go down that parade route without giving my station the boost of recognition it deserved. I ran toward the back of the mini van and opened the hatch door. Inside were a megaphone, some sunglasses, and a box of station bumper stickers.

"Norm, get out of the van. Shaman, come here. Make it quick!" I said, grabbing the items from the car.

"Dookie, what are you doing? Oh, man!" The Shaman threw his arms out to cover me since I had just taken my shirt and jeans off.

I peeled the stickers and placed them all over the front of my bare body: arms, legs, neck, chest.

"Norm, get my backside! Shaman, get my legs!"

"Man, I ain't touching any of that. What's gotten into you? Are you crazy?" Shaman cried.

Norm finished the assignment without complaint and hopped back in the van. "It's freezing out there! You are going to die!" he shouted.

"Trust me, Norm. Anything beats the sweltering heat of a pink bunny costume!"

The Shaman looked me in the eyes for reassurance. "You do know what you are doing, right? Right, Dookie? Randy said to just drive the van and wave. That's what you told us. Remember?"

I put the sunglasses on my face. "That's right, Shaman. We are doing just that. You guys drive..." I placed the megaphone over my mouth and aimed it at his face, "AND I'LL DO THE WAVING! MERRY CHRISTMAS, HO HO HO!!"

****

" 'Parade Prance Has DeeJay in Hot Water,' " read Randy as he quoted the front-page headline of the *Coeur d'Alene Herald* the next day. I sat in his office with my head bowed and my hands under my thighs.

" 'A Coeur d'Alene radio deejay is in the dog house for spreading the wrong sort of Christmas cheer in Friday's Festival of Lights parade. Dookie, a.k.a. Aaron Traylor, drew stares and sparked complaints when he strolled down the street clad only in bumper sticker-covered boxers and a Santa cap.' "

I turned my head sideways to get a better look at the upside down picture of me on the top of the front page. I looked cute in a Santa cap, I thought.

Randy snapped the newspaper down to glare at me from behind his desk, then continued, " 'The KHIT-FM microphone man stopped occasionally to do a jolly bump and grind for the sidewalk crowd, which included parents with young children.' "

There was a long silence. Randy stood up and faced the window.

Uh-oh. I'd been here before.

"You know something? I was a lot like you when I first started out."

Oh no.

"I'd do anything just to get noticed, but I must admit, I've never done the things you have done. You are out there, Dookie. You are totally out there!"

I finally looked up to catch his eye. He walked toward me and leaned over my chair. "I'll be willing to bet you something, because I'm a gambling man."

"Yeah? What's that?" I flinched.

"Once the dust settles and the community moves on to bigger and better things to complain about, this will be the best promotion this radio station has ever put on. Any news is good news, in my opinion."

I heaved a sigh, thinking that he was on my side.

I was wrong.

"But let's get one thing straight, Dookie," he said, shaking a finger in my face. "Pull a stunt like that without my authorization, one more time, and you are fired quicker than I can say the word 'fired.'"

I looked toward the floor once more.

"I give you a lot of freedom, Dookie. Almost too much freedom. No one else in this industry would ever dream of giving his disc jockeys this much freedom. I have half a mind to take it all away from you."

Randy turned and walked toward his leather office chair, where he sat down again.

I didn't dare look at him as I waited for the gavel to fall.

"But, I won't," he decided.

I squinted at him in wonder.

"I'm crazy to keep you on board," he went on. "This town both loves you and hates you now. That's why I'm keeping you around. You keep walking that fine line and you'll soon have the highest rated show in this market!"

"Randy I'm…"

"Don't say you're sorry! Just get out of my office and enjoy your Christmas. But…don't talk about this episode on the air Monday. Just pretend it didn't happen and move on. You've got a bigger test coming up next and I hope you don't fail me. I've got a lot riding on this rave you're throwing, and now, so do you."

I stood up and aimed for the door.

"Dookie…"

I turned toward him as he threw the newspaper on his desk. "Do NOT fail me!"

Chapter Twenty-Three

I never thought the art of turntable mixing could be so demanding. There were times when I'd get so frustrated that I'd have to just step away from it, shake it off, and then try again much later. Thank goodness my teacher was very patient with me. He'd make me just sit there, listen, and watch. It was helpful that he broke it down with simple actions and words for me. I would have been lost without him.

Listening to music the way The Shaman did changed my way of listening to music forever. Never do I hear a song, now, that I don't try to think of another that is compatible with it. While others are singing along to a hit on the radio, I'm humming an entirely different song over the top of it.

It's quite annoying, really. I can never just enjoy the original piece; I always have to be mixing something else into it.

It amazed me to learn that practically every song in current dance music follows a simple mathematical pattern. Some alteration every thirty-two beats moves the song along. Listen to any House or Hip Hop track and you'll know what I'm talking about.

The Shaman used Sir Mix-A-Lot's "My Posse's on Broadway" for his demonstration. Starting with the first beat, he counted thirty-two more, then showed me that the next thirty-two are instantly layered with a new hi-hat, a deeper bass line, or even a catchy vocal. The pattern repeats itself until the end of the song.

It's the DJ's task to add in another song's beats to sync up with the existing track that's playing for the dancers.

I learned quickly that timing is everything. After he matches the beats of two records in his headphones, a DJ throws in the first beat of the song he wants to add, and then, after the appropriate set of thirty-two beats from the first record, he slides the cross fader to play both songs at once. And *voila*! Mixology!

But definitely not as easy as it sounds.

We're not pushing play on a CD here, folks. This is a level of DJing that requires serious concentration and a wealth of talent and skill. (Not to say that radio announcers don't have their own, different sort of work cut out for them, too.)

I find it funny that dancers will straight get into a DJ's face and demand his total attention to put in a request. You don't see people do that to guitarists and drummers while they are on stage! For some reason, people at clubs think that all the DJ is doing is waiting for the song to end, so he can push play on the next track.

So not the case!!

Most weekends I would sit in the booth, as instructed, and with a second pair of headphones, I'd listen to what the Shaman was going to mix in. I gathered many of the basic techniques by simply observing.

I don't think I was allowed to touch the turntables for at least a month, when my teacher thought I was ready.

Along the way the Shaman taught me several other valuable mixing tricks:

1) A DJ should never scratch over vocals:

AUUUUGH! How irritating! DJs should always respect the artist first and foremost. They should scratch or sample only when the beats are minimal - in order to add flair to monotonous parts of a song.

2) A DJ should keep the sound consistent:

The last thing a DJ wants to do is let the dancers HEAR when a song is ending; that gives the partiers the option to leave the dance floor. Also, loud, distorted volume results in many blown speakers.

3) A DJ should minimize trainwrecks.

Trainwrecking (causing matched beats to slip) is like fingernails on a chalkboard.

And the most important rule of all:

4) A DJ should read the crowd:

This is the whole reason behind the "look up" concept. Shaman certainly took his own advice; he looked up from his mixer each and every time he dropped a record, to analyze the dancers' body movements. He was like a body language gauge. If the crowd grew tired of one style, he'd switch it up-tempo to keep the vibe alive.

In summary, a DJ shouldn't selfishly play only the music he or she likes, unless the dancers are really getting into it.

The dancers always come first. If you play for the crowd, they will return to dance again another day.

****

With all the learning and work I was doing, at the station and on the turntables, it was too bad for me that this particular day started abruptly early...

Chapter Twenty-Four

Mullet Man was at it again on the other side of my apartment wall.

All we need is music, sweet music
There'll be music everywhere
There'll be swinging swaying records playing
Dancing in the street
Oh it doesn't matter what you wear
Just as long as you are there
So come on ev'ry guy grab a girl
Ev'rywhere around the world
They'll be dancing...They're dancing in the street

"Please Lord!!! AHHHHH!!!!!!!!!" I pounded on the wall but it was hopeless.

"I hate David Lee Roth. I swear he's the anti-Christ," mumbled Shaman. He rolled over on the couch to see that I had covered my ears with my pillow. "Dude, how do you sleep with that?"

I threw the pillow at the wall and jumped out of bed. "I can't! I just can't!"

I slammed the bathroom door hard behind me, then swung it halfway open and poked my head out "Hey, man. You better not be trying to sleep, because if I'm awake, *you're* awake. Get up!"

"I will...I will. Just wake me when you get out of the shower. How are we supposed to throw this party tonight with only four hours' sleep, anyway?"

"We'll manage. Get up, wuss!" I slammed the door, then slammed it a few more times to get the message across.

"I'm up! I'm up! Dang, you are definitely not a morning person, are you, Dook?"

****

After five months of practicing my hour-long set and two months promoting on the air and on the street, I learned that the fairgrounds committee had given only four hours to set up inside their flower exhibit building. That didn't give us much time at all.

Fortunately, enough club kids showed up early to help load in the speakers and hang lights, anything for free admission into what had been labeled "Spokane's Largest Rave Ever."

The building we rented was indeed legal, licensed security guards were to arrive an hour before the insured event, and the place was hazard free, with all the proper entrances and exits. Still, we gave it just the right kind of atmosphere. Dark, moody, yet industrial. Hard concrete floors, just right for dancing; high vaulted ceilings with an enormous catwalk suspended in mid-air, perfect for people who wanted a bird's eye view of the performers and dance floor.

The very first thing our crew did was inflate a bouncy castle and build chain link cages, inside of which four professional dancers would writhe and grind on each end of the main DJ booth. Plus, we fenced off a huge section outside the building so people could relax in our outdoor chill area. It was filled with tents, love seats and another small DJ set up. These were all my ideas, something new and different that the Spokane ravers hadn't seen.

"Man, Dookie. I've never seen anything quite like this before," said Randy as he stood in the middle of the dance floor, craning his head all around. "I'm surprised that you were able to put this together, under the projected budget, even. I must admit, I am impressed."

"You'll be happy to know that I just got off the phone with the ticket box office. We sold just enough pre-sales to cover the cost of what you put into it," I said with a smile. "The rest is strictly profit."

"Fantastic!" he replied, as he watched The Shaman designating points for the security guards to monitor around the building. "I'm outta here, Dook Man. Looks like everything is under control. I'm proud of you."

"Leaving so soon?" I asked.

"You know, I'm too old for this sort of thing. I'll stand out like an overprotective parent. I'll see you in the morning." He headed for the exit, straightening a sagging KHIT banner before departing.

The hour passed quickly as I sat behind the turntables, sorting out the records that Shaman had let me borrow for tonight's performance. I couldn't control my shaking hands as I filed through the unorganized pile, and I became all the more nervous when I saw the flood lights dim and a wave of teenagers enter the building.

The Shaman tossed me a thumbs up. It was time to begin.

I cued my first record, positioned the cross fader under my sweaty fingers, and took a deep breath. Eyes closed, I threw the record into motion.

I heard the music in my headphones, but no sound projected from the tall speakers on either side. I panicked, waving my arms to catch The Shaman's attention. He hopped onto the stage and looked down at the mixer to see what was wrong.

He smirked as he placed his hand on my shoulder. "It might help if you turned up the master volume." He leaned into my headphone to listen to the record that was playing and spun it back to the first beat.

With a quick, impressive scratch, and the volume now cranked up to max, he set off my first platter and the bass from the tracks. Acid House beats began to resonate throughout the building.

"Just relax, you'll do fine. Concentrate and don't forget..."

"Look up?" I yelled.

He laughed, "You got it. Rip it up, Dookster!"

****

My first few mixes were lousy. Every time I attempted to match the beats they would fly off sync quicker than I could correct them.

Shaman had warned me that it wasn't going to be easy mixing in this environment. I had mixed on the same exact sound system and turntables inside the club's enclosed booth before, but with them transplanted into a much larger space with concrete walls, the sound carried differently. It bounced to the other end of the room and shot back toward the stage, causing the rhythm to be a half-beat off.

I soon got used to it by placing both headphones over my ears.

109

Normally, it's best to have one ear free to mix with the stage monitor, and the other to cue the next record, but I was able to hear the music in real time, doing it this way instead.

Occasionally I'd catch myself getting too wrapped up in the mix and I'd look up to see the crowd peeling slowly away from the dance floor. I counter-attacked by tossing on a record with a different style or beat, just like The Shaman had taught. Each song I blended brought the energy higher and higher.

I programmed my set to start slow and progressively build to insanity. The crowd jumped and cheered as I raised my hands and drummed along to each build-up, making them dance even harder.

The mixing was awkward and not as smooth as I wanted it to be, but I played the right kind of music to keep the majority of the crowd grooving and shaking.

I even saw The Shaman dancing in the crowd. I must have been doing a good job, because I'd never seen him dance at the club, ever. Even though he had heard this music time and again, tonight he couldn't resist joining in.

****

I looked beyond the huge gathering of people, hoping to see one particular face. I prayed that Rachel had heard the promotions on the air or picked up a flyer and recognized my name. She was the one with whom I wanted to share this moment of glory, but it looked like I'd have to settle for everyone else.

By the time my last record finished and another local favorite, DJ Ryan, took the stage to replace me, I noticed that the building was already at capacity. In less than an hour, we had easily doubled the number of people who had attended Revive, and I noticed the line outside was at a stand still, with people begging to get in. Security was keeping a close eye on the main entrance and the fencing to make sure no one weaseled in without paying.

I went outside to cool down, my heart still racing from the enormous adrenaline rush. I crawled onto one of the comfortable couches in the chill room, where DJ Parafyn scratched over down-tempo hip hop instrumentals to set the mood for a mellow atmosphere.

I'd been up since 6:30 that morning and had been going non-stop since. Though there was no way that I was going to get a nap, it did feel good to rest my eyes.

"There you are! I was asking for you at the door, but they didn't know where you ran off to," a familiar voice called from beyond the chain link fence. "Hey, man. How come we ain't VIP? Our names are not on the list!"

I turned to see Halo and Eddie attempting to climb over the high barrier.

"Yo! Get down from there. I'll meet you guys outside. What's up, Ed?"

Eddie looked like death warmed over. His lanky 6'3" body barely had the strength to hold the 160 pounds he was carrying. He slouched, his XXL T-shirt drowning his unhealthy frame. Halo looked almost as pathetic, but carried himself with a swagger, instead of a limp like Ed's.

It took me about five minutes to fight through the crowd, but I soon greeted my long lost friend with a hug. Eddie's ribs poked into my stomach and I could feel his bony shoulders under my encircling arms.

"Man, you guys just missed my set! I had them in the palm of my hand the whole time!"

You spin now? Will wonders never cease!" Halo turned to face the line of people still waiting to get in. "Quite the party you got here. Geez, I wonder who inspired you to put on something like this." He slurred as he spoke, obviously flying high. "You look tired. Need a pick-me-up?"

I noticed that Eddie hadn't said a word since arriving. I remembered that when he was spun-out he always got real quiet. Eddie winked and glanced toward his pocket, directing my attention to a little baggy of powder he pulled half way out of his pants.

"Come on guys, you know I don't do that stuff. Put it back in your car. They are searching people at the door."

Halo's eyes bugged out. "You got security frisking people? This is a joke! You ain't keepin' it real. You ain't keepin' this underground. You've totally sold out! That's what you've done!" He groaned, "This is no rave, Dookie! Where are the chaperones and the spiked punch bowl? Where's the piñata? This I gotta see!"

He aimed toward the front of the line.

"I'm not letting you in," I mumbled

Halo turned on me. "What do you mean, I can't go in? Who do you think you are? Man, ever since you went on the air with that Royal Flush garbage and that horrible mix show, you've acquired quite the attitude. Thinking you're all that and a bag of Frito-Lays. As for The Shaman, he can't mix a glass of Tang!"

"You're high, Halo. I won't let you go inside and disrupt the party."

He dug his finger into my chest. "You idiot! If it weren't for me, this party would never have happened. I inspired you. I..."

"Is there a problem?" The Shaman interrupted. "Don't make me hop this fence and regulate."

Halo took a step back. "This does not concern you, Mix Show Meister. This is between me and Mr. Sell Out."

"Everything cool, Dookie?" The Shaman asked, as he stood there, unflinching.

"It's all good, man. He was just about to leave."

Halo grabbed Eddie by his shirt and turned for the parking lot. Then he wheeled around again, almost falling over.

"We could have made a great team, Dook!" he hollered. "Now that you are a turntable DJ, I could book you for one of MY parties. With your enthusiasm for the music and my underground style, we could really show Spokane how it's done. Something to think about." Then, "Come on, Eddie, let's leave this high school bash. I can think of something I'd like to flush."

Eddie looked sadly at me and mouthed, "I'm sorry," before following Halo back to his car.

"Dookie, come on inside," Shaman said. "Halo's not worth our time. Just forget about him. I already have."

Although the party was hopping, my insides were twisting. I tried to enjoy the rest of the evening, but was too distraught by what had happened.

By morning my nerves were so on edge, all I wanted to do was tear down, load the stuff into the back of the rental truck, and head for bed.

Chapter Twenty-Five

Randy showed up at the fairgrounds at 9:30 in the morning to pick up the cash till. Once again, he stood in the middle of the dance floor.

"This place looks like a tornado hit it!" he said, as he surveyed the soda cans, cups and various litter strewn from one side of the building to the other. "Well, so much for the damage deposit. How did we do, my hard-working zombie?"

I was jealous, because, while I had been up all night, I was certain that he'd had his full eight hours of sleep. I approached him with the cash drawer. "It's all there, Boss. Count it. Two thousand tickets paid for at the door, ten bucks a head. You got twenty thousand grand pure profit. Not to mention the pre-sales at Ticket Master."

Randy opened the box and handed me my share. He looked thrilled, but for some weird reason, not as thrilled as I thought he'd be. "Dookie, what can I say..."

"You can say, I am THE MAN! That's what you can say. Dookie is the man. Yeah!"

I slumped down onto the concrete floor and placed my head in my hands to rest for a moment.

"You need sleep," Randy observed. "You worked hard, Dookie. Take tomorrow and Monday off. You earned it."

At this, he turned to leave, then paused. "And, oh yeah...come into my office Tuesday so we can talk."

Something in his tone left me cold.

****

I woke up Tuesday refreshed and ready to take on the world. I couldn't believe that I had slept through not one, but two mornings of Mullet Man's blaring music. I guessed my body needed more rest than I'd thought.

I recalled brief moments of Sunday evening and all of Monday, when I regained consciousness only to stare at the TV and then fall right back asleep.

I arrived at the station early, hoping to receive even more praise from my boss and my co-workers for the successful event I had thrown. But as I walked through the halls, I could sense a dark cloud hanging over everyone I encountered, especially Randy.

"Dookie, come into my office," he said.

I sat in the chair before his desk.

"Something wrong, Boss? Everything all right?"

"I...I...Dookie...?"

I leaned forward. "What? Say it, Boss. What did I do wrong this time?"

"It's...it's. All I can say is we tried. But we had no choice. We had to do it."

I ran a million thoughts through my head, trying to figure out what he was about to say. The newest ratings weren't supposed to be out for another two weeks, so it couldn't have been that. My Royal Flush was gaining a steady following, and the calls, I thought, were intriguing and entertaining. The mix show was always on point. And we both knew that the party was a humongous success.

I kept quiet and waited for him to explain himself.

"We are changing the format again."

I shot him a confused look as he made his first eye contact with me since I had walked into his office.

"Um...I...but. To what?" I stammered. "What are we...? Why? I'm lost here."

Randy lowered his head, looking defeated. "We are going hard rock."

I bit my lip and thought for a moment. Then I replied, "Well, that's not much of a stretch for me. I can still push the envelope with that kind of format. We will have to can the mix show; that's gonna be a bummer. But, hey, I can adapt. Right? Yeah, I can make the transition. No problem. Is that it? Ah, no worries then. Whew! Man, for a second there I thought I was being fired."

I nervously laughed and hoped for a smile from Randy's troubled face.

The door to Randy's office opened as I was still fixed on his eyes, looking for some kind of assurance that everything was fine.

"What's he still doing here?" words came from behind. "I thought you were going to call him yesterday!"

I nearly fell out of my chair when I recognized Johnny's deep voice.

Randy looked up at him helplessly. "I couldn't do something like this over the phone, Johnny," he said. "This needed to be done face to face."

I got out of my chair and put my hands in front of me to stop Johnny from getting any closer.

"What needed to be done *face to face*?" I fumed. "Randy? Dude! What is he talking about and why is he here?"

"Dookie, we sold the radio station. I'm sorry. I didn't want to tell you like this." Randy turned his eyes away in shame.

Johnny leaned against the wall, a smirk on his face. "Just watch the Dookster," he quipped. "The tears will start flowing any second now."

Randy gritted his teeth. "Hey! Knock it off, John. Let's be civil here."

Johnny was wrong. This time around I wasn't going to cry. I was much too angry to even feel like crying at that moment.

"So, it's like that, huh? Randy? I can understand where you are coming from. I don't blame you. Sell it if you have to but...but sell it to our DIRECT COMPETITION?"

"I'm sorry, Dookie. Upper management couldn't turn down the figures that these guys offered. It was too good for them to pass up. Believe me, I tried not to let this happen. I've battled this for months, actually figuring if I worked hard to make you the best you could be, we would be able to stand on our own two feet. Ironically, it backfired. Becoming the best only made them come at us with a higher bid."

I glared at Johnny, who was still grinning from ear to ear. I got in his face and stared him down.

"Wipe that sappy smirk off your face, Johnny," I snarled. "You know what? Here's my opinion, whether you want to hear it or not: you lost! Straight up! You knew that in the upcoming ratings I would have smoked you, but rather than fight clean, you guys whipped out your wallet and settled this outside the ring. You lost. Plain and simple. Out of my way!"

I forced myself around him to get to the door. Once outside, I poked my head back into the office to find him pursing is lips and shaking limp wrists to mock me.

"You think I'm just going to shrivel up and die?" I growled. "You have not seen the last of me, Johnny. Mark my words!"

Chapter Twenty-Six

It was 1:30 in the morning. Since our party, my schedule was all out of whack. I envied The Shaman, because he was able to fall asleep on the couch without any trouble.

I wanted to wake him, to ask him for more advice. Earlier, he had taken me out to dinner and tried to calm me with reassuring words. He was certain that I'd get back on my feet in no time. Still, his expressions of friendship and kindness weren't enough.

I wished that I could have called myself that night and flushed my own problems down the pipes.

I wanted to walk to Inspiration Point and pray, but I figured park security would kick me out after hours. Instead, I crept into my bathroom and just stared at myself in the mirror for the longest time.

I got to thinking about Saturday's party. I had proven to myself and everyone else that I could hold my own as a promoter and as a DJ. I had pulled off the biggest "rave" this town had seen, and I had torn the roof off the joint with my opening set. I began to realize that I didn't necessarily need a radio station behind me to succeed. It had taken only seconds to generate a reaction from that dance floor, whereas I had to wait months for ratings, to learn what my radio audience thought of me and my show.

I wanted to continue to throw my own events. But there was one problem: money. I didn't have any. The Shaman wanted to funnel his money back into his club and was not interested in constantly throwing raves, so he was out of the question. No one else I knew had the needed revenue to pull off a small scale house party, let alone another massive event.

Then it dawned on me: there was one person who could help. Problem was, though I still respected him, I hated him.

Halo's effect on me was hard to grasp. His attitude was self-righteous, he was arrogant and a liar. Yet I was mystified by his charisma. I will never be able to explain why I found him so fascinating. Any wise person would have pushed him aside. I, on the other hand, held him high on a pedestal, yet wanted to take him down from it.

Looking back, the only rational explanation I can come up with is that it was a subconscious thing, implanted in my system when I was ridiculed by those jocks at my middle school. They despised me, yet I wanted desperately to fit in with them. Enough to try to beat them at their own sport.

Was that why I was swaying toward Halo's offer to play at his parties?

I had a serious inner conflict, as I continued to stare into the bathroom mirror. Should I settle for a mundane nine-to-five job, and be just like everyone else? Maybe I should go to school and get an education.

Maybe Johnny was right! I should look into another profession. I was being eaten alive by this one.

Or should I hone my skills as a performer, and take this passion for music to the next level? I had promised Johnny that I wasn't going to shrivel up and die. If I backed out now, I'd be lying to him and myself.

Then and there I decided to distance myself from the juvenile "Dookie" nickname and find a stage name that was something more in tune with who I was becoming. Time to wipe the slate clean. If I was going to perform at Halo's events I was going to do it by my own rules, without the past to haunt me.

My name was Aaron. Sometimes I forgot that, having let the story of my life's biggest humiliation define me as "Dookie." Dookie had served me well, turning that awful embarrassment into a triumph, but it was time to move on.

Aaron, however, was not a good DJ name: too plain, no flair. My new handle would have to be something that would stand out in lights. Something different, but with meaning.

I walked out of the bathroom and decided I'd give myself some time to think about a name. I knew, however, that regardless of what my new moniker would be, Halo was the only source I had to help me get where I wanted to go. That wasn't going to make me rest any easier.

I stretched out in my bed again, tensing up every muscle, releasing, and then breathing out to relax myself. I counted to one-hundred and back three times. Still, no luck. Hopeless.

It was 2:00 AM. I wanted to turn on the TV, but I didn't want to disturb The Shaman as he snored away on the couch.

Some people enjoy running water to help them sleep. Some babies are soothed to slumber by the sound of a vacuum cleaner. The Shaman prefers dead silence. I enjoy hearing conversation right before I pass out.

I quietly grabbed my walkman out of my desk, the same old walkman I'd used since junior high. It still worked perfectly and still served to drown out the world around me.

I put the headphones on and tuned into the talk show channel on the AM dial. I figured if anything was going to put me to sleep, it was going to be a boring conversation about the economy or politics.

However, my interest was stirred when I caught Art Bell's coast-to-coast late night program. I loved this guy, always will. Sometimes I'd catch portions of his show as I commuted back to Spokane from Coeur d'Alene after my own radio shift, and that was when I got hooked. I listened every chance I got. Since I was quite the night owl, I was able to catch his show often.

He talked about the strangest stuff: UFO sightings, alien abductions, ghosts and demons, you name it. If it had anything whatsoever to do with the paranormal or supernatural, he was all over it. Yet, he usually kept his opinions to himself and allowed his listeners to draw their own conclusions as he presented the creepy evidence.

Art was just wrapping up a segment on crop circles when I tuned in that morning. I listened to the commercials and visualized Norm at the station, segueing back into the program from the studio control room.

When Art returned from the break, he began with a disclaimer. This was a first. I had never heard him actually warn his audience this way before. Art claimed that the sound byte he was about to play was both frightening and disturbing. Anyone with a weak heart should turn off his or her radio for twenty seconds.

I thought about switching to another station, not because I was "chicken," but because I wanted something to put me to sleep, not freak me out. By now, however, I was all too curious.

Art explained that what we were about to hear had been recorded by a geological team who were drilling holes into the center of the earth from Siberia. According to the story, after they had drilled several kilometers through the earth's crust, the drill bit had suddenly begun to rotate wildly. They soon realized, by their fine-tuned gauges, that the temperature at the core was much hotter than previous drillings in that region had indicated. The resultant discovery was so terrifying that the scientists were deathly afraid to continue with the project.

In an attempt to track the shifting of the earth's different layers, and to help explain why the heat was so intense, the team had extended a high-sensitivity microphone into the deep, dark shaft. What they heard turned the logic-minded Russian scientists into trembling wrecks!

They claimed to have drilled straight into the GATES OF HELL and to have heard human screams from the condemned souls held there! The traumatized scientists were afraid they had drawn the evil powers of Hades up to the earth's surface!

Art gave one final warning to his audience, but the way he had built up this intense story as terrifying enough, without the sound byte. Glued to my walkman, I turned up the volume to get a better listen.

Art paused briefly and took a deep breath. I could tell that even our intrepid talk show host was a bit freaked by his own delivery. He pushed play.

Shivers went through my entire body as I witnessed the unmistakable sound of a human female voice, screaming in pain. It sounded as if she was being tortured in a concrete basement, her limbs pulled from their sockets and knives twisting in her abdomen.

Although this one voice was pre-dominant, I could also make out, in the background, the screams of thousands, perhaps millions, of tormented souls. I could have sworn I heard whips cracking and the sound of a deeper, evil voice barking orders. The hair on the back of my neck stood straight up.

Those twenty seconds were the most horrifying of my life.

Yet, I had to hear it again.

Fortunately, I had connections.

"Norm! I'm glad you answered! Norm...Norm?"

Aside from his answering the station request line with the call letters, there was absolute dead silence on the other end of my phone.

"Norm! This is Aaron, er...Dookie! Hey, bud, you there?"

By that time, The Shaman had awakened and glared at me to keep it down.

I whispered, "Norm, I can hear you breathing. C'mon man. Did you hear that? Tell me you heard that!"

"...I heard it."

"Norm, everything all right? You're cool, right?"

"...That was...that was..."

"I KNOW! Some freaky stuff! That's why I'm calling! Tell me you recorded that. Please tell me you got a copy of that!"

The Shaman grumbled and threw a couch pillow at me.

"Listen, I gotta go, but I want you to mail me a copy of that sound byte. Find my address in the employee listings, if I'm still in it, and get that to me as soon as you can."

"... ...k... ..."

"Thanks, Norm. Good work. See ya."

Chapter Twenty-Seven

You know I, I found the simple life, weren't so simple, no
When I jumped out on that road
Got no love, no love you'd call real
Got nobody waiting at home
Runnin' with the devil
Runnin' with the devil
Runnin' with the devil
Runnin' with the devil...

"Unbelievable!" I yelled into my pillow. Emitting a deep growl, I squeezed a corner of the bed sheet until my hand cramped up.

The tormented cries from the depths of hell had replayed in my head, keeping me awake the whole night. When the sun began to fill the room the next morning, I just lay there in my bed, staring at the alarm clock, waiting for Mullet Man to strike. Like clock work, this guy.

No matter how many times I'd banged on the wall or yelled through the air duct into his apartment, my attempts to attain peace and quiet had always been futile. This was it. I had had it up to here with Van Halen at 6:00AM. I was fed up with playing Mr. Nice Guy. Mullet Man was going to pay the price...right now!

And of all the songs to be playing this morning! *'Running with the Devil,' how appropriate!* I thought, as I reached for my shoes and jeans. *It's like I'm living a nightmare!*

I stood up, but fell to the floor while attempting to put my jeans on too quickly. It was the loud thud that woke up The Shaman.

"Duuude, can't a guy get some sleep around here?" he snarled, his eyes still closed.

"Trust me. After this morning, we will both sleep much easier. Where are the keys to your van?" I said as I regained my balance and curled my upper lip. Body slamming my chest into the wall with each amplified word, I screamed, "This guy has NO IDEA WHO

HE'S MESSING WITH!" .

Shaman mumbled and blindly felt around on the floor, his hand flopping around like a landed fish. Finally, after a few sightless attempts, he peeled one eyelid open and found his shoes. He pulled his keys out of the left one and tossed them to me, totally missing my hands.

"I'll be back," I grumbled as I bent over to pick them up. I slammed the front door on the way out.

I sped through my neighborhood at 50 MPH, not slowing for any intersection or stop sign. I was on a mission and nothing was going to get in my way. Not even the morning joggers whom I narrowly missed with the back bumper.

The screaming Sounds of Hell would not stop no matter how loud I sang the verses that had awakened me. Those horrifying cries still lingered in my head, overlapping the Van Halen lyrics. I figured if I could at least take care of Mullet Man, I would regain some control. That would be a good start.

I laughed wickedly as I saw the joggers flip me off in the rear view mirror. "Oooooh, running with the devil!"

****

The Shaman was in the shower by the time I got back from The Jungle that morning. I had been gone for an hour but my neighbor's music was still blaring through the walls.

I had hauled some heavy sound equipment from the club and I wiped the sweat off my face as I positioned the last piece in the middle of the living room floor. "All right, Mullet Rocker, let's get one thing straight," I muttered, while plugging the final RCA into the back of the borrowed mixer. "Mess with your neighbors all you'd like…but don't mess with a DJ!"

I cued up the track and slid the cross fader into the center. With the record paused under my fingers, I could already feel the deep vibration from the needle begin to shake my living quarters. JBL three-way stacks and two bass bins jacked into a two-thousand watt Crown Amplifier faced only a few inches from the wall that stood between us and the enemy. With one flick of the wrist, I set off a quake that could be felt not just through the walls but throughout the apartment complex, across the street, and around the block.

Clamping his hands over his ears, Shaman leapt out of the bathroom in nothing but a towel. His wet feet lost traction and he landed on the hard kitchen floor.

I laughed and banged on the wall to antagonize Mullet Man even more.

Between the bass throbs, I could hear a muffled rattle. It seemed to be coming from my front door.

"HMMM...I WONDER WHO *THAT* COULD BE?" I chuckled loudly, as The Shaman hustled back into the bathroom. I assumed it was Mullet Man ready to admit a humble defeat.

Unfortunately, it was my landlady from down the hall. "TURN IT OFF! TURN IT OFF RIGHT NOW!" she shouted, while kneeling down to rub her aching toes. Her shoes had made deep gashes in the wood of my door as she had tried to get our attention. Apparently she had been kicking and banging on it for quite some time.

I stopped the record and placed the needle in its resting position.

The landlady pushed her way inside and limped across the room. She shook her finger at me viciously. "Aaron! What's gotten into you? Do you care to explain why..."

"Sorry, M'am. Just a mis-wire. It won't happen again. Trust me," I said in a reassuring voice. I ushered her politely out the door.

The Shaman leaned out of the bathroom. "Aaron? What *has* gotten into you? I've never seen that look in your eyes before. Are you OK?"

There was a slight pause before I erupted in sinister laughter again.

Chapter Twenty-Eight

A month later, I sat in Eddie's trailer on the shabby couch where I had rested my head far too many nights. I didn't miss Eddie's surroundings, but I did miss him and there was no way I was going to miss his Revive Two after-hours party.

I had just rocked that rave with what one kid called a "phenomenal" performance. It was my first time in front of a packed dance floor during the peak hour of an event. I could almost feel my ego inflate with each nod, hug, or high five I received as I walked through the crowd after my set. I figured that, at an after hours party, I'd surely receive more praise.

The entire event, partnered by Halo and myself, had been an incomparable success. No busts, excellent new venue, lots of pretty girls, and a righteous vibe that kept them all dancing until the last record spun down.

Did I mention the pretty girls? That's what I was waiting on more than anything else, since Halo had promised to bring some over after tear down. I would have invited all of them back to my own pad, but I wanted to keep a low profile around my landlady since the Mullet Man war.

I looked at my watch. 8:30 AM. I could hear the traffic start to pick up on the nearby freeway. Families waking early, I thought, loading the wee ones into their mini vans or station wagons to take in a healthy breakfast before worshipping and praising God at their churches. And here we were in a dingy trailer park, waiting for our party from the night before to continue. My breakfast? A bottle of Evian and a pack of Camel Lights. Worship and praise? They would be abundant here, too...all directed at me!

Eddie sat Indian style on the floor. It looked like he hadn't slept for a week. "You sure you's gonna be's able to's stay awake this mornin' ff..f.for the Bettys, yaaahh bro, you know? Cool?" he stuttered, as he kept picking at an infected sore on his neck.

He was starting to sound like he had invented his own language. I called it tweaker talk. It's when you do so much meth that your brain begins with one thought and your mouth starts to form the sentence, but your mind hurries ahead to the next thought. This causes the end of a sentence to have nothing to do with the beginning.

Still, I knew what he was trying to say.

"They are on their way, Ed. We will just hang, you and me. Just like old times, right?"

This was the first time in about a year that I was able to be alone with Eddie. Generally, we were at some loud party where he'd be on one end of the room trying to score and I'd be on the other, mingling with the promoters and other DJs. I figured now was as good a time as any to bring up some concerns.

"Yo, Ed. I've been meaning to ask you. How are you doing?" I tried to catch his wandering eyes to get his undivided attention, but that was impossible. He kept shifting his concentration from one thing to the next. "Ed, everything cool? You seem a bit distant lately."

He stopped grinding his teeth for a moment, only to put a pacifier in his mouth. Then he continued to gnaw away again. A few seconds later, he snapped his head up to look at me briefly. "Yeah, iss all good. Tryin' t..t..to maintain, represent. Iss all good. Just goin' through tough times, tough times, man. Yeah, tough. Word is born."

Eddie looked out the window and started to twitch involuntarily. His eyes squinted. "Dang, man. It be bright up this place. Get some shade up in heyah. Sun shine no mo. Eyes be buggin' out."

He got up and pulled the shades together to block the morning light. Poor guy couldn't stay seated for too long. Always had to be doing something active.

All this moving around, picking at his skin, grinding of his teeth, was starting to wear on my last nerve. I finally gathered strength to stand up and grab him by the shoulders, demanding his attention. His face was toward me but his eyes were rolling around too fast to focus on me.

"Listen, Ed, if you ever want to talk, I'm here for you. We're friends and friends are there for one another, always."

Eddie pushed my hands away and turned his back to me. I could hear him clenching his teeth even tighter. "What is this? Man, j...j...jus' back off. I'm cool. It's cool. We's all good. Ain't no thang. I can handle my own business. Word."

"Eddie, chill. You've just been acting different lately. That's all. I just want to see if there is any way I can help you. Quit getting so defensive!"

"Help me? Help ME? Man, you was the one that needed help. What about you's crashing h..h..here when you's needed a place to crash? W...what about...what about..." Eddie threw his hands up and spun around to face me, "AH! Ferget it! If you wanna help, you can help by cleanin' my house, you can, you can...you can pay my electricity bill...they's gonna shut it off if I don't pay it by Tuesday. You...can...you...can...keep my Grampa from going in and out of the hospital all the time." He thumped on his scrawny chest. "You can find me a woman who loves me for my inner beauty! Find me a job, get me a car that runs. Yeah, that's how you can help."

I could see him fighting back tears, but he'd never admit it. I had never heard this kind of animosity in Eddie's voice before. He was trying to hold it all in. But each suppressed tear was another problem he chose to deal with on his own.

I could hear Halo's sports car peeling around the corner toward Eddie's house. I would have continued with this opportunity, but not with everyone else in the same room. Some other time, perhaps.

"Eddie, just don't forget I'm here for you."

I went to sit down on the couch and Eddie went into his room.

The front door suddenly swung open. "What's up, you freak?" greeted Halo, as two slender beauties pulled out from under his arms. Both of them rushed toward me to pull me up from the couch.

"Hey! It's him! It's DJ O2-N! Halo told us you'd be here! We really wanted to meet you after we saw you perform."

The red-headed one wore a sexy latex tank top with laces that criss-crossed in between her full breasts. The brunette had the eyes of an angel, a devilish grin, and a body to die for. Both were stunning and although their ragged looks indicated they had been partying all night, it didn't stop them from pressing themselves close to my side.

"Oooh, he is tall! You were right, Halo," said the red-head.

"And cute, too!" replied the brunette, as she ran her fingernails up and down my arm.

One of the girls was wearing Rachel's Elizabeth Arden perfume. When I closed my eyes I could just imagine her back in my arms.

"Well, sit down. Get comfortable," directed Halo. "Dookie. I want you to meet Priscilla and Shakina, two of your biggest fans."

Both were amazing creatures, even if their eyes were dilated and their mouths were twitching from all the ecstasy in their systems.

The girls rested their long legs on mine and put their arms around me as we sat on the couch together. One would tease me by twirling her fingers though my hair and the other stroked my knee delicately.

"So, it's Aaron, right? Why does he call you Dookie?" asked Priscilla.

My face turned as red as her curly hair. "Long story."

Shakina giggled as her fondling got closer and closer to my groin. "Silly, he's the radio DJ we used to listen to. Remember? You called in and wanted to flush your ex-boyfriend? This was the guy you were talking to!"

Priscilla's eyes became even larger and she drew her legs away, twisting her body upright to face me. She flashed me a big smile and then seductively slid herself on top of me, wrapping her legs around my waist.

"Ooooh, that WAS you! I thought you had the sexiest voice."

Both her hands were now free to rub my scalp, while Shakina's lips lightly ran up and down my goose-bumped neck. I closed my eyes and smiled while enjoying the sensation of four hands caressing my body. Priscilla continued, "All right, shy boy, answer me this. What does O2-N mean?"

"Oh, I can answer that!" Halo smiled as he cracked open three beers and handed them to us. He sat across from us, swigging his own, and began.

"We were trying to figure out a good DJ name for 'The Artist Formerly Known As Dookie' and came up with the scientific symbol for oxygen. O. 2 represents the number of As in his name, or two airs, then N. O2-N. Get it?"

"Ooooh! Hey! That's clever. O2, plus N equals AIR-N! I got it now That's very unique," squealed Shakina.

"Hey, you asleep, down there?" Priscilla asked, as I drifted off into a relaxed slumber. I wanted to stay awake but was too comfortable.

"He looks tired. It's been a long day for both of us, hasn't it, Dookster?" Halo moved to the couch beside me and the girls. "We got a little something that might help you out, don't we ladies?"

Priscilla and Shakina looked sideways at one another and giggled like little school girls. I opened my eyes when I felt Priscilla's hands leave my head. She reached down to the laces on her tank top and untied them. Her hand slipped into her black bra and pulled out a small vial of meth. She never lost contact with my eyes as she calmly twisted the cap off and dipped her fingernail into the yellowish substance.

"Listen, Halo, girls…I…"

"Look at it like this, Dookie," Halo interrupted, as he began rubbing Shakina's shoulders. She moaned with pleasure. "You work hard. We work hard. Promoters and DJs have a different clock than most. We are always the first to show up for a party and the last to leave. Others work 9 AM to 5 PM; we 5 PM to 9 AM. It gets hectic. A normal person, such as yourself, can't survive off adrenaline alone. Think of this as two things: first, a reward for doing a great job behind the decks last night; second, a tool. Utilize this stuff sparingly when you need a boost. When you are throwing a party you NEED to be alert or you're gonna lose control."

Shakina leaned in closer to breathe heavily into my ear. "Go ahead," she purred.

Priscilla placed a fingernail under my nose. The smell of the stuff alone was enough to wake the dead.

"Yeah, but look at Eddie," I interjected, as I put my hand over hers.

"Eddie? Eddie doesn't know when to quit! That's the difference. Like I said, use it sparingly and you won't get hurt. Just look at me. I do it every weekend and I'm just fine!" he argued, while chewing on his bottom lip.

Priscilla pressed in tighter against my chest and whispered in the other ear, "It's all right. I'll take care of you."

"WE will take care of you," Shakina coaxed.

"Close your eyes and take a deep breath," Halo instructed, while Priscilla closed one of my nostrils.

I did.

Moments later the burn kicked in. The pain was intense. It felt like battery acid behind my eyeballs. I began to cough hard, as the disgusting sensation crept down my throat.

I pushed Priscilla away to grab a water bottle sitting on the coffee table. I chugged as fast as I could but the burning wouldn't stop.

"Here, do this." Halo took a toot, laced a few drops of water into the palm of his hand, then sniffed it into his nose. "It will help, trust me."

The water calmed the irritation slightly. I sat back and waited for something to happen while the girls took their share of the substance. When they finished doing their rounds, Priscilla arched her back and placed the half empty vial on the coffee table.

She put her weight back onto my body and nuzzled her nose into my quivering shoulder. She kept sniffing to get the residue into her system.

I guess she didn't need water. Must have been a pro.

"Mmmm, I can hear your heart racing," she moaned. "I love that sound."

Chapter Twenty-Nine

Invincible.

If there is one word that best describes what it is like to be on meth, that would be "invincible."

On top of the world, stronger, faster, smarter.

After the girls left, Halo and I hopped into his sporty Volkswagen Jetta and snorted rails all the way to the mall so we could distribute the pre-flyers for our next big party.

Sure, Revive Two had just happened last night and we had passed out a whole bunch of invites at the party, but that didn't stop us from spreading the word to the rest of the city. Even if we hadn't slept in over twenty-four hours.

"Hey, Dookie," Halo shouted, keeping his voice one notch higher than the speakers blasting in the back seat, "you got a needle and thread?"

I grasped the car door handle and leaned into the curve, which he took at breakneck speed. "No. Why?"

"Because I'm RIPPED! Wooohooo!" he screamed as he launched the car over a parkade speed bump. He grabbed the emergency brake. "Hang on!" he yelled as he fishtailed the back end of the car and spun it perfectly in between the two yellow lines of a parking spot, dangerously close to the cars on either side.

I used my knees to pry my hands off the door handle.

He lowered the emergency brake and put the car into park.

"Hee, hee!" Halo beamed. "I always wanted to do that!"

****

"Hey, we'll be leaving these flyers on your checkout counter," Halo said to the Gap sales manager, while he tried to maintain a professional demeanor. That's difficult when you're having trouble standing in one place, scratching your cheek because it feels like you have bugs crawling on your face. The yuppie manager, who looked to be in her late thirties, pulled her tinted sunglasses down to read the fine print. After a brief look at the flyer, she raised her head and addressed us with a snooty tone, "Sorrrrry. Can't."

"Are you serious? We bring them here all the time. What's the big deal?" argued Halo.

"Store policy," she quipped, turning around to fold a stack of jeans.

"Let me see it," I said.

"See what?" she asked, focusing on her project.

"I want to see this so-called 'store policy.' Who specifically says we can't?"

No reply.

I hate being ignored. I walked up behind her and knocked her tightly folded stack of jeans to the floor. I had never been the kind of person to do something that rude, but I was full of enormous energy and irrational emotion. My mouth was speaking faster than I could think.

All I knew was that something had to be said, because this was the fifth store in the mall that had turned us away that afternoon. "What is this? Some conspiracy?" I growled. "We've dropped off countless flyers in this mall before. Now, you and everyone else are saying we can't."

"Who the heck do you think you are?" she shrieked. "Bend over and pick those up! Right NOW!"

By then everyone in the store was riveted on us. A couple of dressing room doors opened slightly so the occupants could see what the commotion was all about.

"We know exactly what you're doing at these parties," the manager snarled. "All night dancing in some undisclosed location where underage kids go when they lie to their parents about where they are going, so they can experiment with the latest club drug. What do they call it now? Crank? Crystal Meth? Whatever it is, it looks like you boys are enjoying a little too much of it right now. It's written all over your faces. Just get out. Jaime! Call security."

As Halo grabbed my shoulder to maneuver me out the door, I continued to swing my arms, knocking over clothing displays as I stumbled backward.

"You just don't get it!" I hollered. "No matter how much you try to suppress us, we will only come back stronger and harder! You and everyone else in this place just want to hold us back! We have a right to dance!"

I tripped over a jacket rounder and Halo caught me before I fell to the floor. I grabbed a coat hanger and held it high above my head like a banner. "You can take away our right to promote, but you can't take away our FREEDOM!"

I tossed the hanger across the store and bailed out the door.

Four security guards spotted us from the other side of the mall, and it appeared they were relaying our location by two-way radio for back up. We pretended not to notice while we hurried our step. The food court between us and the rent-a-cops was a sufficient obstacle, giving us a second to plan a defensive maneuver.

"There are more on the way," I told Halo. "They'll probably circle us and close in. What do we do? If they question us, they're gonna know we're high!" I panted as I moved my feet faster.

Halo, with his short legs, tried to keep up. "I haven't a clue, bright guy. You started this, you finish it."

I bristled. Perhaps I had started this particular incident, but I never would have done anything like this, had I never met Halo. There was no time to argue, however. We quickly arrived at the intersection where the food court diverged from the stores. I looked in both directions. Handing a brick of flyers to Halo, I said, "Let's split up. We'll cover more ground that way."

"You can't be serious!" he objected.

"We've come this far, we might as well go the distance. I am not leaving until people here know about our event. Blanket this place and meet me at the car in five minutes."

Halo shrugged and grabbed an even larger stack out of my backpack. He darted down the east corridor, while I aimed for the west wing. "You're crazy, but I love it! See ya, Dook! Don't get caught!"

By the time we went our separate ways, security was about seven stores removed from where I was. Being on the second floor of the mall was helpful since all I had to do was sprinkle flyers over the guardrail as I ran along the mezzanine. I tossed hundreds of flyers overhead and watched them drift down to the main floor. It was literally raining flyers...beautiful!

Hundreds of curious shoppers picked them up from the floor or caught them in mid-air. I ran on, leaving a trail in my path. Each store entrance received an explosion of paper promotions. I didn't care where they landed - on people's heads, in shopping bags or baby strollers. Just so long as word got out and *I* got out of this without getting arrested.

Halo was having more than his fair share of hurdles to pass; it looked like most of the security had gone down his hallway.

My destination was finally in sight. The parking lot entrance was only a hundred feet away. Security guards were rushing to catch up, fighting through the oncoming crowd, which kept them a safe distance behind me. Although they were far from nabbing me themselves, that didn't mean that they didn't have other resources to stop me.

After receiving orders on his two-way, one janitor lunged his broom in my path, hoping I would stumble over it. My sped-up reflexes allowed me to hurdle over the sweeper's offense, while tossing another stack of flyers into his face to distract him.

"Nice try!" I laughed.

I was the first to make it to Halo's car. About ten seconds later, Halo came barreling through the lot, nearly out of breath. He unlocked the car doors with his keyless remote and motioned for me to hop in the passenger seat.

The yellow siren lights of a mall security truck cast a flashing glow behind Halo's sprinting shadow. He had made it to the car with just enough time for us to escape.

They couldn't touch us once we were off their property. The chase ended when we merged into street traffic.

We kept under the speed limit and coasted to a stop when we came to a red light far away from the mall.

Halo took a deep breath, then slapped me across the face with the back of his hand. "You are getting crazier by the minute, man.

Freaking crazy!"

"Hee hee!" I giggled. "I always wanted to do that!"

Chapter Thirty

After my marathon weekend, I slept sixteen hours without interruption. Once awake, it was difficult to convince my body that it was a good idea to get out of bed.

There was a conflict between my brain and the rest of my body.

"Hand, move," my brain would demand.

"Nah, don't wanna," the hand would reply.

"Legs, stand," my brain would order.

"No... we're too tired," the legs would reply

I finally just decided to give up, and pass out again.

"Yo, man. Rise and shine! It's six in the evening," The Shaman commanded as he leaned over my bed, shaking me until he saw signs of life. I blew the bed sheet off my eyes to acknowledge him.

"I must have dozed off. How did you get in?" I groaned, while my limp hands found my face and rubbed my eyes.

"I let myself in. You didn't answer the phone all weekend. What's wrong with you? Your eyes, they're all..." He paused.

I turned around to curl up under the comforter. I didn't want to submit to examination.

"What time is it?" I asked, trying to change the subject.

"I just told you, man. Six."

"In the morning?"

"Aaron, it's six in the evening! TUESDAY evening," The Shaman roared. After a moment of dead silence, he swiftly ripped my blanket off. Then he grabbed my shoulder and made me face him while he sat on the edge of the bed.

"What's gotten into you, Aaron?" he asked, shaking me again. "There's something different about you."

I struggled out of his grasp and propped my weakened body against the headboard. Avoiding eye contact, I looked down toward my feet, which dangled off the end of the bed. My mind was mush. I couldn't think of anything to say.

"Listen, I heard about your little fun and games at the mall. Everyone is talking about it. Stuff like that is going to land you behind bars. You know that, right? Hanging out with Halo is just going to get you into more trouble like that. He's a bad influence. I thought you already knew this. Why did you have to be an idiot and start working with him?"

"I owe Halo everything," I declared. "If it weren't for him, I'd be nothing." I crossed my arms and stared straight ahead.

"Correction. If you keep hanging out with him, you WILL be nothing. Aaron, you have to realize that if you continue to hang with him you'll get yourself in deeper. You have to trust me on this. Can't you see he is just using you? He is banking on your popularity to bring more people to his events. That's all! I've seen people like him come and go ever since I opened the club. They come in claiming to be the next best thing and soon leave because they can't cut it. They either get themselves into too much trouble with the law, the scene won't support them, or they get too strung out to make rational decisions. "

I kept silent.

"He's dragging you down with him. Isn't he? He's got you doing things that you never thought you'd be doing. I'm right, aren't I? I remember that time you saw Eddie outside our event. You hadn't seen him in months. You could barely recognize him. He was too far gone by then. I know that shook you up. I could tell. I saw it in your eyes."

The Shaman nudged my chin up with his knuckle. "I can still recognize you. It's not too late for you."

I jerked away again. It was all I could do to keep him from seeing the tears that beaded up on my lashes.

"You know, they say when people are ashamed they tend to avoid eye contact with other people," he said glumly.

"I am NOT ASHAMED!" I yelled, catching him off guard with the volume. I, too, was a bit taken aback by my own projection. I tensed up, nervous and edgy. It was like my body had kicked into defensive mode to compensate for any weakness. I was, after all, invincible.

"Where do you get off assuming anything?" I yelled louder, as

I leaped off my bed. "You don't know Halo. You apparently don't know ME! How are you able to see into the future and predict what will and won't happen? I think I have a better idea of what my destiny is than you do. And what makes you think he is using me? Huh? Huh? Maybe *I'm* using *him*! Maybe I know exactly the kind of people I need to surround myself with to take me to the *next level*."

Shaman looked offended. "Oh, I see. I get it now," he said. "Were you just using *me* to get to 'the next level'?"

I was stunned. "No! It's n-nothing like that with you," I stammered. "I trust you, I really do. I don't trust Halo, but I...If you...I..." Flustered, I plopped back down on the edge of the bed.

"You are not making sense, Aaron. Really, I am trying to understand. This is so unlike you to blow up like this. This is not the Aaron I know. Maybe I was wrong. Maybe I really never knew you."

"Shaman, listen..." I wanted to say something to keep him there, but I was too slow to come up with anything clever. He was the only good thing left in my life, but I couldn't find words to tell him so.

"No, you listen. Aaron, I can't support you any longer. If you are going to continue to get high every weekend and raise all hell with Halo, then do it. But do it without me. I'm sorry, Aaron...Good bye."

The Shaman stood up and crossed the room. He opened the door to leave, but took another look at me before departing, and nearly tripped over a parcel left in the hall. He kicked the box inside and shut the door.

Hell was about to be raised.

Chapter Thirty-One

"That is the creepiest thing I've ever hear heard! Play it again! Play it again!" said Halo as he sat on the edge of his chair.

"Yo...I'm gggggetting...I got goose bumps, yo," Eddie stuttered as he chopped up lines with his library card on Halo's coffee table. "I've got a bbbbad ffffeelling about this."

Once I received Norm's package, the tape of Art Bell's "Sounds of Hell," I immediately wanted to share it with my friends. We must have played the sound byte five-hundred times at Halo's pad that night.

We loaded it into his sequencer, looped it, played it backwards, equalized it and processed it time and time again to see if we could detect any clues that the Sounds of Hell might be a hoax. We found nothing. All we did was convince ourselves of its horrifying validity.

If anything, the screams were now clearer and we could actually hear the crackling of enormous fires in the distance.

I leaned my head back on the sofa to keep the temporizing water from leaking out of my nostril. I was getting used to meth's burning. It didn't hurt nearly as much now.

"I think we should play this at a party and see what happens," I suggested.

"Ha! That would freak everyone out," Halo agreed. "Hey, check this out...it's a track I created on this Frooty Loops music maker program."

Halo opened a folder on his desktop computer and clicked on the .wav file. The instrumental song was deep and dark. Chunky rhythms, crashing cymbals, ferocious bass lines. I could sense that Halo had made this song when he was in a really bad mood.

"Now, here, get this."

Halo rewound the DAT tape and cued up Art Bell's introduction. He recorded the broadcast into his computer and, after a brief editing session, was able to cut out a few of Art's key words and phrases: "THE GATES OF HELL,"

"PARANORMAL," "SUPERNATURAL." Then he began to record the screaming into the Frooty Loops.

Halo yelled over the stereo monitors, "I'm gonna play my track in one bank. Then I'll put Art's voice into another. And we will put this screaming in as the breakdown of the song. That's just what it needs! Heck yeah! I'll have to mess with it a bit, but I think we could make a slammin' track with what we've got now."

His eyes brightened like shining black beads. "I should make this a track on the record I'm releasing!"

"Hey, what's that b-beeping n-n-noise?" asked Eddie, as he glanced around. "I haven't heard that p-p-part before."

"Neither have I. What is that?" I questioned, as I put my ears closer to the speakers. "You hear that, Halo? It sounds like a....phone."

I walked toward Eddie and the noise kept getting louder. "Yo, fry brain, you're getting a call," I said, rapping Eddie's skull with my knuckles.

"At three in the...three in the morning?" He arched his back and reached into his pocket for his cell phone.

"Hello? Hey..." Eddie's embarrassed smile quickly faded. "I'll be right there."

Halo turned the volume down on the monitors. "What? What is it?"

Eddie stood up and grabbed his jacket and keys. "My Grampa...he's..."

I helplessly embraced my friend. "I'm sorry. Eddie, I'm sorry. He fought a long, hard battle."

Eddie sobbed on my shoulder for a few minutes. He shook and squirmed under my arms while I held him close, my shirt soaking up the tears and nose drippings.

He soon peeled away and, without saying a word, left for the hospital.

I sat back down, next to Halo. We shared a moment of silence, and then came the questions.

"What is he going to do now?" I asked. "His Grampa

supported him even when he moved out on his own. He can't afford to pay rent, let alone the payments on his car. What is going to become of him?"

"Your guess is as good as mine. He's on his own now," Halo responded, while clicking and dragging the files on his computer.

Suddenly, he directed his attention to the coffee table.

"Oooh, look! Eddie left his stash behind! Cool!"

Chapter Thirty-Two

...ring...ring...ring...ring...ring...ring...

I had a difficult time telling if it was the ringing in my ears from the blaring JBL monitor tweeters at the party the night before, or the phone.

My eyes cursed the sun coming through the curtains, so I blindly fished for the cordless with one hand, while wiping drool off my chin.

"Hmmmrrg...He...Hell...Hello?"

"Is Aaron there?"

I popped my sore neck back into place and rolled over onto my side, the handset dangling between my cheek and the saliva-soaked pillow. "Yeah..."

"I'm looking for Aaron."

"Yeah..."

"Aaron, please," a female voice said impatiently.

"Who is this?" I grunted, squinting to ease my pounding headache.

"I'm looking for Aaron Traylor. I was told he could be reached here. Do I have the right number?"

I opened my eyes partially. "It's...It's me, that's me. I'm..." I was quickly interrupted.

"Aaron? It sounds nothing like you...are you kidding?"

My remedial skills were quickly jump-started. I shot upright and sat on the edge of the bed. "Rachel?"

"Yes! Wow! Aaron..." Her excitement made my heart race. "Wow."

"Wow," I repeated before a brief, awkward silence.

"Yeah, wow...I mean, man! You are one hard guy to get ahold of. I started to freak when I didn't hear you on The X, but then I caught you on that new station. Then again up and disappeared. I called the station and they wouldn't give me your number."

"You listened to my show?" I asked.

"Of course, silly. How else was I going to keep tabs on you? You were so good on the air. Sometimes I'd pretend you were talking directly to me." She paused, then said softly, "I miss hearing you."

I was still in shock that I had Rachel on the other end of my phone. "How did you get my new number?"

"It's the strangest thing! I saw Eddie at Riverfront Park. It was good to see him, although he looked awful. I think I caught him right after he'd been crying. He was mumbling something about his Grampa. Is he OK? Are...you OK, Aaron?"

"I...I...I need to see you," I whispered.

****

I spent three hours prepping myself. Men should not primp this long; it borders on femininity.

I must have cleaned, rinsed and inspected every cavity, every inch of skin, and every hair on my body, and then cleaned them again. For some reason, I felt grimy from head to toe, no matter how much I soaked under the shower nozzle.

I think I put on a little too much Drakkar Noir before I bolted out the door. Hopefully the brief walk down to the Elks Café in Browne's Addition would air me out.

I was late. My heart was about to leap out of my ribcage. I was so nervous with anticipation, that I'd had to calm myself down with another rail before I left the house. Not too much though, just enough to get my edge back.

My walk turned into a sprint.

When I turned the corner to look inside the café window, I caught her glancing down at her watch. I had to stop and stare before I went in.

She didn't see me, but I saw her. I put my hand on the glass and just gawked. Her hair was longer. Her new outfit was trendy and classy. Her skin was like a porcelain doll's. She was a million miles ahead of me in style and grace. I felt reluctant to even go in.

I was in love. I was in love with that girl!

As I continued with my innocent voyeurism, I saw her reach

145

for her purse and rise from the booth. She tossed a crumpled napkin onto the table and quickly headed for the door.

I ran toward the entrance and caught her before she left the building. We stopped just inches away from each other.

No words were exchanged, just an interlocking stare. Mine of love and absolute surrender, hers of pure frustration.

"You scared me. I thought you were going to pull another one of your legendary no-shows," she said.

The aroma of her perfume seemed to neutralize my Drakkar. What memories her scent evoked!

"Please, come sit," I said, trying to motion her back inside.

"No, I feel like walking. I've been sitting here too long." She started to walk away, then turned. "Join me?"

We rounded the corner and made our way to the nearby neighborhood park. We didn't talk until we found a bench to sit on.

Her long hair reached the top of the wooden backrest. It was even shinier than I remembered.

She looked at me long and hard before speaking. I could tell she was holding something in. "I don't recognize you," she said sadly.

She stared deep into my eyes. I felt as if I were being put under a microscope, so I turned my head down and stared at my crossed legs. "I couldn't recognize your voice earlier," she went on, "and now...I just don't recognize YOU."

Still fuzzy headed, I immediately jumped to the defensive. "Yeah, well I *am* different. I'm different because I don't have the aura of success and popularity anymore." I shrugged. "Listen, for years we were just good buds, hanging out with Eddie. The romance came when I got to be a big shot radio jock. That's what finally attracted you to me, so now that I don't have it any longer, of course I look different."

Rachel let these words sink in. It seemed she was about to spout off, but she managed to address me in a calmer voice than I expected. "You know something? Sitting at that café, waiting for you to show up, reminded me of the time..."

"Don't say it…I don't need to be reminded."

"No, Aaron, listen to me. Because what I'm about to say is not what you expect. Understand that yes, yes I did get a bit excited when we were going together to the prom. Yes, my girlfriends asked who I was taking and I couldn't help but describe my date as Aaron. Aaron, Dookie, the DJ, you know, THAT guy." Her eyes were big and round as she relived her adolescent enthusiasm.

"Sure, I wanted to make them envious," she admitted. "But that was just the girl in me. Girls are attracted to successful, popular guys. However, I would like to think that I learned a hard lesson. I am more woman, now, than girl: a woman who knows better than to base a potential relationship on such standards alone. Now I know that it's not what a man does that's most important, but how he treats me and how he can love me."

The more I listened, the more I had difficulty keeping my body from squirming around on the bench. I was twitchy, edgy.

She continued to stare me down.

"You look so different, so…thin. Are you getting much sleep? You look anxious."

"I'm fine."

I wasn't. My eyes blinked rapidly and my teeth were clenched so tightly it would have taken a crow bar to pry them open.

"I feel strange about all of this," she sighed. "This is not how I expected this to turn out."

I leaped off the bench and fired back, "Why? Because you were expecting the man you fell for on that dance floor? Like I said, I'm not that guy anymore! I don't have the clout I used to, the kind of clout that won the girl in you so long ago. But I do see through YOU! And you know what you are? Someone who would like to think that she's all grown up and is looking beyond the glitzy exterior, but who still has that little girl on the inside begging for a man with credentials."

"Aaron! You have it all wrong! Listen! I could have called you at anytime when my parents weren't looking. I could have been one of those DJ groupies who calls in begging for her song to be played. But I didn't."

She looked away. "I let you run your game and listened from afar. I listened for a voice, the voice of Aaron, *my* Aaron that I knew forever. Occasionally I would catch bits and pieces of the real you, but it was soon drowned out because you were hiding behind your stage name."

She frowned. "Don't think I don't know what you are about now. I see the flyers, I hear about the parties: O2-N is simply your latest alter ego. But I don't like either of them, Dookie or O2-N. Ever since you chose this profession over me..." Her eyes glinted with tears. "...I have never been the same."

Her voice trembled, as she asserted, "In fact, I *resent* what you do for a living now. It used to be all new and exciting. Now that I've had a chance to experience what's underneath the exterior, I'm not sure I find what you do so glamorous anymore. And what's worse is knowing that you are so self-absorbed that it's taking a toll on your health."

She leaned close and studied my pale face. "Answer me. Are you OK?"

Invincible. I was invincible.

I was too strong to let her know what I felt back at the café. I could not let my guard down.

I think back to that day often. That was one turning point that I question and analyze to this day. If I had surrendered, I could have gone back to being the man Rachel needed. I could have abandoned my selfishness and everything could have been perfect. Perfect for me, perfect for us. We could have danced again, someday.

When I did not reply to her sincere concern, she stood up to leave. "You're right, Aaron," she said at last. "You are no longer the boy *or* the man I cared for. I know this now that I see you."

I reached for her and she looked into my softened eyes.

Where was that crow bar when I needed it? I needed to speak my heart right then. When I did not, tears made their way down Rachel's china doll cheeks.

With another sigh, she loosened my grip and slipped away.

The last I saw of Rachel was her sad departure down my Victorian street. Before I managed to apologize, I was talking to the lingering scent of Elizabeth Arden.

Chapter Thirty-Three

As I try to recall the ensuing period in my life, things become hazy. Days blend into weeks, weeks into months, and many months. I've lost track of dates and times; it's difficult to remember the sequence of events, or details along the way.

But I do remember a few things. For one, at this point, I was in deep.

Two determined minds worked around the clock to find locations for each new event, to promote with flyers and posters, set up decorations, schedule DJ lineups, negotiate talent fees, create VIP lists, organize "peace patrol" security teams, etc., etc.

Sometimes it was all too much, yet it felt like it had to be done. No one else was going to do it. Those who tried to help failed miserably. Our constituents were the strongest and our parties were the best. We loved our work and the kids loved us for doing it.

When the music started, everything always felt better, and it seemed worth every effort, even if we lost money and sleep in the process.

Over the course of a half-year, Halo and I threw twenty events. Our raves attracted a minimum of eight-hundred to one-thousand kids every weekend. For a small city like Spokane, that was an outrageous number.

After a while, the police began to catch on to our growing enterprise. Our persistent nemesis, Sergeant Conrad, and his tactical team were definitely on to us, and the department used its power to try to wipe us off the map.

Special events facilitators and warehouse owners with whom Halo and I had established relationships were contacted directly by Conrad himself, convincing them not to host raves anymore. I personally had seen many officers at our parties. We didn't invite them. They crashed in unexpectedly.

Patrol cars would roll into the parking lot to have a "look around." More often than not, the cops felt the need to come in, usually it twos, rookies pulling the red eye shift, who would wander through the crowd and point flashlights directly in kids' faces. If they found something not up to code with the building, they would break parties up by telling everyone, admittedly in a non-hostile fashion, to go back home. If anyone got in trouble, it was either the venue owners or the kids busted for possession, not us.

Soon, locations were becoming harder and harder to find. The authorities cornered us indirectly. Since they restricted a majority of the venues in town, it seemed our only option was to go underground.

Yep, I was in deep for sure. Literally. We now resorted to hosting party after party *underneath* the dirty, industrial streets of Spokane.

More and more often, access to our raves, the only way in and out, was through a steel grate in a dark alley downtown. "Just raise the grate," we instructed our guests, "climb in and close it so cars can roll right over it."

In the bowels of the earth beneath was a gruesome basement with no windows, no running water. It was our only choice, we reasoned.

But, it had its merits. The rugged stone walls made even the smallest sound system concert quality.

Yes, we told ourselves, this venue was superb for raves. We packed the place with kids every weekend, without the absent landlord even knowing it. Not only was it free, but it was located where cops least expected it. Right under their very noses!

While the Spokane police tripled surveillance on Riverside Avenue, the Saturday night cruise strip, Halo and I ushered kids into our alley, half a block away, and sent them down through the pavement to join our underground bashes.

It was amazing that things went so smoothly. Eventually, however, there was one party that didn't go as planned.

****

Halo and I had always invested our personal resources into our events, gambling our rent money and drug allowance into the budgets of the parties. Often we came up in the red. But, we hoped to double or triple our investment with the *biggest party ever:* DJ Halo's Record Release Party.

Despite our new underground motif, we had to promote above ground as much as possible. That's why...

Eddie and I had once again crossed enemy lines. This time we flew in below the radar, low enough to buy us some time so we could distribute our product...

Chapter Thirty-Four

"Wait your turn! Just hang on!" I yelled over the line of fifty kids impatiently waiting in the dark alley. "We are over capacitated, so you are just going to have to wait until some people come out!"

"How much longer? My friends are down there," a girl in angel wings and glitter inquired as I held the anxious teens at bay.

"Your guess is as good as mine, sweetie. You are simply going to have to wait your turn. Look on the bright side. At least it's not thirty degrees outside."

On the contrary, it was a very hot and humid summer night. Earlier that day we had all suffered through one-hundred degree weather. Dragging the equipment down the steps had been absolute torture.

And now I was stuck with the responsibility of keeping the peace above ground, because Eddie had failed to show up on time. He needed to sleep, he'd said, soon after we narrowly escaped authority at the mall. I knew he was depressed by his Grandfather's death, but he seemed incapable, anymore, of reliability.

"O2-N! What's the hold up? Why are all those kids up there?" Halo shouted through the steel grate below. I looked down to see him tucked away in the shadows, sparking a cigarette.

"Yo, there's way too many people down there; they can't fit in!" I yelled back.

"Nonsense! There's plenty of room down here," he retorted. "Besides, we don't want to attract attention in the alley. All a cop has to do is drive by and we're done for."

I knelt down to address him more closely while he crawled up the ladder.

"Halo, I'm not going to argue about this in front of everyone. The place is packed like a slave ship down there. I'm not going to risk these kids' lives just so we can make more ticket sales!"

Halo puffed on his Camel Light, making a smacking noise every time he pulled the filter out of his mouth. This was a sign that he was getting anxious. It was a good thing that my entire body weight was situated on top of the grate; there was no way for him to come up and get in my face.

He wrapped his fingers around a few of the metal rungs and glared ferociously at me. "Fine. FINE! Just answer me this question. What would Eddie do in a situation like this?"

"I'll sh-sh-show you how I'd handle my biz. W-w-w-atch this. Watch this."

I spun around quickly to see Eddie's arms open wide as he ran toward me. I stood up to receive his bony embrace. Instead he passed right by me and started flapping his arms like a bird.

His eyes were all bugged out and it looked like he had seen a ghost.

"What's this boy's trip, yo? Homeboy be buggin'!" quipped a baggy-panted patron sucking on a lollipop.

Eddie flapped his arms violently at everyone in line. Each person he approached hid behind the next to get out of his way.

"Eddie, what is this? What are you doing?" I muttered.

"Get dowwwwwn! Get dowwwwwwn! Get on down!" Each time he said that phrase, his legs buckled and he swooped low to the ground.

"Yeah, boy!" the lollipopper laughed. "We'z about to gets down as soon as DJ bouncer let's us inside, yo!"

"He sure is a good dancer!" admired the girl in the angel wings.

"No, listen!" I barked. "I think he's trying to tell us all something. What is it, Eddie?"

He swooped toward me and tackled me against the wall. We slid down the rough bricks onto the street, where he pinned me to the ground and held my head to the concrete.

"Sssh. Listen," he whispered, pulling his police scanner from his back pocket and putting it to my ear.

"...fz...13-82 in progress on the corner of Sprague and Riverside...fzz...Copy, I'm heading east bound, ETA:30 seconds...fzz..."

"Holy...it's the cops! They're coming through the

neighborhood.   Quick! Duck behind the dumpsters! Everybody! Get down…NOW!" I screamed.

Within seconds everyone had thrown themselves against the wall and crept down behind the large disposal units. One guilt-ridden kid emptied his backpack-full of mushrooms into a garbage can before slipping into the shadows.

Suddenly, red and blue lights cast a fearful glow across the entrance to the dark alley and the sound of high-pitched sirens froze everyone's movement.

A police car was approaching at a fast clip; we could hear the roar of the engine blast right past the alley.

"What's going on?" Halo inquired, as he raised the grate to look onto the street. "I don't hear them any more. Where did they go?"

"P-p-prostitute sting on Sprague Street," Eddie replied.

"That was too close for comfort!" Halo yelled. "Get everyone inside." The freaked-out partiers, still hovering in the dark corners behind the dumpsters, rushed to comply.

I crawled out from under Eddie's weight, as the kids opened the grate and scurried down the ladder. Halo ushered them down the musky passageway, opened the inside door and blaring music swiftly filled the alley. Then, just as quickly, the music dimmed as the last person entered and the door shut.

Steam rose from the humid basement through the grate and dissipated into the fresher air above.

As I stood up, Eddie brushed off my backside.

"Thanks, bro," I said.

Eddie turned down the scanner volume and crept up off his knees. "Nnnnn…no problemo, no problem, Homie." When he got to his feet, a bag of pills fell out of his vest. He swiftly picked them up and tried to poke them into his pocket, only to find that there was little room in there. When he pulled his hand out, another baggy popped out and fell through the grate.

"That's quite an assortment you have there. And a lot of it, too," I observed with concern. "Planning on sleeping anytime soon?"

"If..I..If I did fall asleep, I wouldn't want to wake up."

I disregarded his comment, motioned for him to follow me, and opened the grate.

"Come inside. I'm about ready to go on," I said. "But keep an ear on the police reports, bro. I've got a bad feeling about tonight. And...give me one of those pills so I can take the edge off."

Eddie handed me three.

Chapter Thirty-Five

The heat was unbearable.

Each time the peace patrol shot off their super soaker squirt guns, the water just evaporated seconds after it made contact with people's skin. I had to slow-tempo the pace of my set to keep the kids on the dance floor. If I played hard house, around 140 beats per minute, my dancers would quickly become exhausted. I stuck with some jazzy disco beats instead, just enough energy to motivate them, but not enough to get them hyped.

Shakina and Priscilla paraded in front of the turntables like slithering snakes. Their eyes never left me. One would gaze into my face innocently while the other would massage her with prickly fingers. The come hither stares were often too much to bear. The girls would occasionally grind up against the speakers, alone or together. Each time they got near they'd brush their bodies against mine. Goose bumps crawled up one side of me and down the other. I melted with each touch. The three ecstasy pills had kicked in thirty minutes ago.

I was having difficulty focusing. Too many distractions can keep me from concentrating on my mixing. It didn't appear that people noticed my blatant train wrecking, because they were fixated on the girls in front of me, or on their own dancing.   Still, I could tell that my work was lousy and I was starting to get paranoid. REALLY paranoid.

Normally, my confidence allowed me to throw the cross fader in the middle, so that both songs played at once for a number of phrases. Tonight, I had to keep one song playing for many minutes at a time to correct and overcorrect my beat, matching in my headphones before I let them hear the blend. But, even the blending was short and without flair, because I was too nervous to perform any tricks. It came off like galloping horses, rather than one consistent beat riding in sync with the other.

The temperature was rising, scorching my brow. My body could no longer manage its own weight. I was swaying back and forth, nearly falling over, time and again.

I motioned for Shakina to hand me the water bottle she was carrying in her backpack. She graciously passed it to me and I took a deep swig. Instantly my gag reflex spit it out. Vodka was not what I had in mind!

The Chinese food I had eaten earlier quickly followed it…all over the record I was cueing up!

I raised the needle and wiped the tone arm off with my shirt, then evenly picked up the platter to keep the gag from slipping onto the mixer. I shook the urp onto the floor and tossed the vinyl behind me.

Shakina tried to hold back her laughter. She managed to mouth the words, "I'm sorry," before I collapsed.

Everyone stopped dancing and stared in shock.

The girls picked me up off the stage and motioned for Halo to replace me.

He already had his headphones on his ears and a record in his hand. Stepping onto the stage, he barked, "Get him some water and put him in the VIP room!"

Halo placed the air-raid horn record on the turntable and turned up the microphone. "Hey," he yelled to the astonished crowd, "I've been told it's much funnier when he's wearing a bunny suit."

****

The VIP room: a murky, stench-filled bathroom, the size of an outhouse, with one dim orange light bulb.

"We are leaving you here. You gonna be OK, sweetie?" Priscilla asked, as she fed me a warm bottle of Gatorade.

I nodded. Since I'd hurled I felt much better. Everything had just wanted out, so I'd let it.

All over the turntable, in front of three-thousand kids!

"Here, hold this drink. We'll be outside in the passageway, getting some fresh air. It's burning up in this joint," Priscilla said, closing the door behind her.

I sat on the toilet lid.

This may have been a strange place to pray, but as I did so, my head began to clear and I started to see outside these walls.

"Why am I here? Why? God! Can You hear me? Why am I here?!?! You wanted me here. Remember the little talk we had? Remember the people You introduced me to and the connections I made with Your guidance and support? All of Your guiding has led me here! Look where I am! Look what's outside, beyond those doors!   Did You or did You NOT help me create all of this...this...this controlled sense of anarchy? Weren't there angels on my side this whole time, watching over me? Where *are* You? Why aren't You answering me when I call for You? Just say something! Allow my ears to be the proof that Your voice actually exists! "

I sat there and waited, closing my mind to the blaring siren of Halo's opening record, hoping to hear something far more significant. And I continued to wait until I was convinced that I was just talking to myself.

I kicked the VIP door open and stepped out into the sweaty temple that Halo and I had built.

About a thousand kids were dancing at a synchronized turtle pace, bobbing slowly up and down. Two-hundred-and-fifty or so were nestled on top of one another in a huge puddle fest on the floor, near the exit to the underground passageway. Kids just melting all over one another, exchanging backrubs and flashing red bike lights in their friends' eyes. One girl smacked her pacifier, gnawing the rubber nipple into shreds. A boy lay on her belly, grinding a glow stick in his teeth like a dog with a chew toy.

Curdles of sweat rolled off each body. In the darker shadows, crack heads huddled together, sharing pipes, or couples entwined themselves in half naked orgies. It looked like everything moved in slow motion as I headed for the passageway.

Once outside, I was somewhat revitalized. The cooler air lifted the sweat off me while I stood with others who shared in the same pleasure. Steam rose from our wet shoulders, into the moonlight that filtered through the grate above.

As fresh air slowly coated my lungs, I had renewed energy. The ex was still in my system, but the sickness had subsided. It was good times from here on out, I thought.

****

I recognized the track that was being mixed inside. It was something I could most certainly bounce to.

I went to the dance floor to release myself, if only for a brief while.

The break beats built to a frenzy and the room's energy started to climb. For the first time that evening, I witnessed transformation on the dance floor. The forcefulness of the aggressive track got everyone on their feet, hooting and hollering as they anticipated the climax.

Just as we were peaking, however, Halo added a surprise to the mix. Craftily, out of nowhere, came the Sounds of Hell.

The jumping crowd landed on their feet and stared straight ahead at the turntables. Cranking a mini disc recording of the Art Bell track, Halo killed all of the lights. The only illumination for three-thousand souls came from the single orange bulb swaying behind the half-opened door of the VIP room.

None of us, including, myself, had ever heard the screams of the damned in such a setting. Nor had I ever experienced them this clearly before.

Suddenly, I had to leave. I had to get away!

I pushed through the inky-black room, wedging between masses of warm, moist bodies. I fought through the bewildered partiers, aiming for what I thought was the passageway and exit.

Hands grasped onto me from all sides, and I clung to them, trying to maintain balance. I felt people, actual people underneath me! I had no idea who I might be stepping on.

I couldn't tell if the screams around me were from the speakers, the now-panicky ravers, or both. Finding no end to the throng, I decided to brush away any body parts that weren't my own and kneel down in a ball to protect myself.

Suddenly, the intelligent lighting swooped over the crowd,

revealing piles of kids atop one another. In their desperation to escape this bedlam, many had tripped and fallen, others scrambling over them in the dark. With the help of glow sticks, some tried to bring order, but their efforts were futile.

Frantic, I shot up out of my fetal position and waited for the smart light to pass over again. As it did, I caught a glimpse of the distant passageway. I aggressively moved with the swarm of kids fighting to get outside. Like asthma victims without inhalers, we gasped for air, once we reached the passageway.

My head was still spinning when I noticed the glare of red and blue lights flickering on the stone wall. To my horror, I realized these were not coming from the dance floor, but from the street above.

"Quiet!" I warned the churning mass in the corridor, as I pointed overhead.   I hastened back inside, pushing against the exiting tide, and, reaching the stage, I flailed my arms to get Halo's attention. He went right on mixing. At last, I pulled the mixer cord out of the power strip and the music instantly stopped.

"What the...?"

I cupped Halo's mouth. "Everyone, quiet! Quiet! Cops...upstairs!"

After the shush had passed to the back of the room, there was dead silence. All that could be heard was panting and wheezing from the audience.

"Go talk to them, Dook." whispered Halo.

"Are you nuts?" I shot back.

"I'm not doing it. You do it!"

"You!"

He grasped my head and mouth with both hands, holding on tightly as he murmured, "You need to go handle this! You are the only one. I froze up trying to get us out of that previous mess with that cop, remember? You rescued us both! Do it again, Dook!"

He kept squeezing until I felt my cranium would collapse. I nodded in wide-eyed fear, hoping he'd let go.

I pushed my elbows into his shoulders and pried myself loose.

Once free, I nearly fell back, but caught myself on the wall speakers behind me.

As I staggered through the crowd, I could hear weak cries for help and whimpers of fear. I tried to reassure our patrons with a calm tone and false words of encouragement.

Once in the passageway, I could hear the sounds of two-ways beeping above. The purr of police car engines was enough to keep the partiers still.

As I slowly climbed the ladder, I could make out the shadows of men in uniform, mace cans, handcuffs and nightsticks in hand. Then, the silhouette of one man in particular, staring down as I got closer.

He stepped off the grate and opened it halfway to duck inside.

Once I reached the top, I was able to recognize this policeman's familiar face.

"Quite the *revival* you got going on in there. Mind if me and my boys come in?"

Chapter Thirty-Six

Each person inside had to pass a thorough inspection once he or she made it to street level. At least three kids, including Shakina and Priscilla, were sent to jail for possession; others were forced to contact their parents to pick them up.

It was the biggest police raid our scene had ever experienced.

All who were left in the underground dungeon were the volunteer sound crew, Sergeant Conrad with three of his assistants, and myself. Somehow Halo had slipped through the inspection. I guess he pretended to be just an innocent partier, not responsible for the craziness below.

"This reminds me of the parties I used to throw," Conrad embarked on a reflective "back in my day" moment. Inspecting the dark room with his flashlight, he said, "My friends and I would rent out an old barn or grange and just whoop it up with folk bands. Man, we brought in some great artists. They'd sing and we'd dance, drink some and watch the sun come up." He turned to me and stepped closer. "But things have changed since my era of partying. All we had was alcohol and maryjane, which was bad enough. But your drugs, nowadays, they kill! They kill innocent kids! You think I want my daughter to come to one of your events and be introduced to this garbage? Do you have any idea what goes into this stuff?"

I shrugged as if I didn't care.

"Did you know that some of the cooks down in Browne's Addition actually piss out their toxins and recycle them back into their product? Bet you didn't know that? Did ya? Think about that when you decide to put some of this stuff up your nose again."

"So, what is this? Are you gonna bust me or what?" I sneered.

"Bust you? Good question. I don't think so. Nobody died, right? You were searched and there was nothing on you, right? You are free to leave as soon as your boys get this gear cleaned out. One thing is for sure, however: you will most certainly NOT be using this facility again."

I leaped forward, but the cops intervened.

"What? This is all we had left! Where will we go now?" I objected.

The sergeant leaned into me between the officers. "Anywhere but here. Not in this city. Not ever again."

He turned to leave, but then spun around to address us one more time . "I'm going, but my crew will be on hand to make sure everything is cleared out and the place is locked up behind you."

After briefly instructing his officers, Conrad grabbed me by my shoulder and pulled me near the exit, away from everyone else. "One thing before I leave, and I want you to listen to me like you've never listened to anyone before. Find yourself, Aaron."

"Find myself?" I muttered.

"Drop this BS and bring back the best DJ this town ever heard, or you will surely suffer the consequences of your actions. Do you understand?"

Those familiar last words gave me goose bumps. He had spoken them to Halo and me on the bridge the day we said we were having a "revival."

It occurred to me, now, that he must have known the lie of that. Why he didn't arrest us at the time must have been an undeserved gesture of leniency.

I could sense in my heart that we dare not test his patience again.

****

Once the last speakers were carted up the cumbersome ladder with thick ropes, I searched the facility for anything we might have left behind. I was the last one out of the passageway before an officer took a padlock to the grate and securely fastened it shut.

I went to my truck, which was parked on a side street, and fished through my jeans for my keys. Once inside, I gave a sigh of relief before starting the engine.

A loud slap on the back window caused me to jump and glance toward the rear view mirror. I saw a large palm pressed against the glass, sluggishly smearing its way down to the frame.

I leapt out of the cab and saw Eddie hunched in a fetal position in the bed of my truck. He was shaking and sweating. His eyes were in the back of his head.

Halo pulled up to the curb and rolled down his window. "Whew, close call. What's up? What is it?"

"It's Eddie! He's overdosed!"

Halo hopped out of his car and peered over the tailgate. "Well...well...well. Looks like someone had a little too much fun," he grinned.

"THIS IS NO TIME TO LAUGH!" I bellowed as I rushed at him, tossed him against his car and clenched his shirt collar tightly. "My friend is dying! Can't you see that? He's a walking pharmacy and you are making light of it!" I pushed him aside, spitting, "You are so pathetic!"

I returned to Eddie and placed a hand on his warm head while Halo slid to the ground.

"You left me to fry down there with the cops, but you are going to help me now!" I barked. "You are going to help Eddie! We are taking him to the hospital. Follow me!"

"Are you serious?" Halo cried. "Man, you really are stupid! Imagine what would happen if we dropped off some toked-out, e-tarded, cracked-out druggie at the emergency clinic. And here we are, just your average every day all-age dance promoters 'helping a friend.' Haven't you had enough authority riding us for one night? Let's get him back to your place. There we can split the profits and..."

"NO WAY!" I yelled as I headed for the driver's side of my truck. I would haul Eddie to the hospital without Halo's interference.

But, before I even had a chance to react, Halo rushed up behind me and ripped my keys out of my hand. Pushing me, he threw me off balance, landing me on my backside in the street.

I could barely blink my eyes before he was in my truck, peeling off for who-knew-where.

Leaping to my feet, I thought to take Halo's car and follow

him. I was relieved to see that the keys were in the ignition, but by the time I pulled away from the curb, Halo was so far away I couldn't be sure where he was headed.

"Probably my place," I figured, remembering his suggestion.

To my dismay, however, my truck was not in my driveway; neither were Halo or Eddie anywhere near my house.

I took off again, this time to Halo's, half-a-mile away.

No one there either!

"Eddie's!" I groaned.

I raced the five miles out of town to Eddie's trailer park and ramshackle dive. There I found my truck sitting idly in the yard.

"Lord!" I begged. "Don't let him die!"

Chapter Thirty-Seven

I sat on Eddie's all-too-familiar couch, cradling his nappy head on my lap and feeding him cold cans of V-8, hoping the nutrients would revive him and stabilize his irregular breathing pattern. I stroked his wooly hair, trying to keep him awake, while Halo paced nervously, smacking his lips on a cigarette.

"He's not getting any better. You know that, right?" he said.

I had called 911 on my cell phone the minute I pulled in the yard and knew where Rescue should come. "The ambulance is on its way," I growled. "Why don't you just leave?"

I propped Eddie's head on a pillow and went into the bathroom. I filled the grimy glass on the edge of the sink with cold tap water to dab on Ed's face, and keep him from sleeping.

As I stood at the faucet, I was caught by my own reflection in the mirror. At least I thought it was mine. I didn't recognize my own face. My cheeks were gaunt and pale; my eyes were bloodshot and there were dark circles under each one. Looking down, I realized that my belt went in two extra notches and my previously form-fitting shirt was draping over my wilting frame.

Way to go, Aaron, I thought to myself. *This time it's Eddie. Next time it'll be you.*

I heard the front door slam and left the bathroom. Halo was gone.

I rushed to Eddie's side and knelt down, holding his clammy hand tight. "Can you hear me?" I wept, as I trickled cool water on his brow.

I buried my head on his chest.

"Aar…"

"It's me, bro. Save your energy, help is on the way."

Tears streamed down my cheeks onto his soiled T-shirt. "You've got to do me a favor, Ed. You've got to fight to stay awake. You are strong. I know you can do this. Fight!"

At last a siren wailed in the distance. "Can you hear that, Ed? They are coming! They're on their way. You're gonna be OK.

You're gonna be just fine!"

Eddie's breathing was becoming more sporadic. I shook him and propped him up so he could fill his lungs more easily. I pressed my head against his chest and waited.

Our experiences together ran crazily through my mind. I remembered him sitting in the driver's seat of his Audi Quattro, chatting on my cell phone to nobody, just so he'd look important. I remembered our escapades in the mall, brazenly passing out flyers; I remembered how Ed had peeked at my worthless answers while we took math tests at Sacajawea Junior High; how he had stood by me the day I was christened "Dookie;" how, as little kids, we used to play hide and seek beneath the church pews after Sunday School.

I held him closer to me, hoping that our cherished memories would keep him alive.

Suddenly there was a bang on the trailer door. I rushed to get it.

"Paramedics!" a uniformed squad member announced. "Where is your friend?"

"On the couch," I replied.

"Is he asleep, sir?" the man asked, hastening with two other medics into the living room.

"I've been trying to keep him awake," I answered.

"Good. Let's hope he IS awake," he said. "If he falls asleep, his pulse will lower and he might not revive."

Suddenly, I remembered what Eddie had said earlier that evening: "If I did fall asleep, I wouldn't want to wake up."

A nurse with a stethoscope bent over Ed.

"How is he?" I groaned. "Is he still breathing?"

The first medic placed a plastic breathing device over Eddie's mouth. He blew into it a number of times and then used both hands to jump-start his failing heart.

I sank to the floor and rocked on my knees, staring in horror at the situation before me.

The medic repeated the process over and over again while the nurse and assistant stood by. Each time the medic breathed into the mask, I'd see Eddie's chest expand, giving me hope.

At last, however, the medic leaned back, pulled the breathing mask from Ed's face, and looked at me helplessly. "It's no use. We tried. I'm sorry."

My heart sank, my bottom lip quivered. I leaned back on the floor to face the ceiling.

The medic looked at his watch. "Mark it down, Dennis. Time of death, 2:32 AM."

Chapter Thirty-Eight

I rested my head beneath my shower nozzle and just let the water cascade down the bridge of my nose and into my mouth. Traces of ecstasy were still in my system from the night before, making my face hypersensitive to the warmth of the water…or was it tears? I couldn't tell.

I had left the bathroom door open so I could hear my front doorbell. I expected it could ring any minute. If it did, I knew better than to think it would be Halo returning to find out about Eddie. After he left Ed's trailer, I would never see his face again.

Nor would I see a dime from the profits of our last rave. He had absconded with all the money.

As far as I was concerned, my half of the profits was a fine trade for him to get out of my life, forever. I couldn't help but blame him for my best friend's demise. If he had let me know where to send the ambulance in time, we might have been able to save Ed.

No, I was expecting someone else could come to my door at any moment. Soon enough, the cops would piece together Eddie's death with last night's party.

I pushed my war torn body through the process of showering. I wasn't going to just sit around and wait for the authorities to arrive on my porch. I would clean myself up and then pay them a visit, instead.

I scrubbed my pale and unhealthy looking skin with a bar of soap, as I rehearsed the things I wanted to say to Sergeant Conrad. No matter how hard I scrubbed, however, I couldn't get the dirt off of me and I had a hard time getting the words right. The dirt had seeped into my pores and found its way into my veins, but I was determined to come clean, in more ways than one.

****

"Sergeant Conrad can't see you now, sir. He pulled a late shift last night and will return on Monday. Please come back tomorrow," said the polite lady behind the Spokane County Court House information desk.

I grabbed my metal jewelry and watch out of the security tray and headed for the exit door. Once outside, I sat on the courthouse steps and rested my head on my hands. I was disappointed that I couldn't see Conrad right then, because I was certain that I was going to forget what I wanted to say to him. Short term memory loss was one thing I had noticed about my current health, besides my weight loss and bags under the eyes.

For the first time in ages, I was Aaron. Just Aaron. No eccentric nicknames, no charming personality-driven facade. Just a boy who had lived his dream to the fullest extent, only to lose the point of what he was dreaming about somewhere along the way.

I had no more dream. There was nothing to live for. I sat and waited for nothing because nothing was all I had. My underground empire had collapsed. My best friend was dead. The love of my life was unobtainable. My state of mind was fragile and weak.

Something had to come from nothing or else my only option was to die along with everything I loved.

If I wanted to be optimistic, I could have said that I had some great memories...of music, lights and people...throbbing bass lines and seas of hands in the air...changing colors on skin and faces that altered in rhythm to the sounds I generated...strobes blasting white onto masses of sweaty people who joyously screamed and bounced to the breakdowns and buildups of my tracks.

But, had all of this been worth the inevitable sacrifices?

My blank stare crossed the courthouse parking lot and landed on the distant Monroe Street Bridge. I sat on the steps, pondering my life, until I decided to wander down that way.

As I approached the bridge, I noticed that the brick wall which Halo and I had painted had all but collapsed. My limbs needed stretching so I climbed up on the ruins and surveyed the broken bricks, wondering if any part of our old sign might still be there.

I kicked around the dirt and stone, but found everything reduced to rubble.

A cold breeze against my back drew my eyes skyward. The clouds were starting to look fierce and menacing. Rain speckled the dry and dirty concrete at the base of the wall.

"Okay, what is this supposed to mean?" I snarled at the heavens. "Why did You bring me here? It's the wall. You wanted me to see the wall, didn't You? It's destroyed; there is nothing left of it. So yeah, I get it now. You brought me here to point out the obvious. Don't think I don't already know that I have failed. I don't need this symbolism to be reminded. What I do need is for You to acknowledge me when I ask for You. I needed you last night! More than ever I needed You last night!"

The rain began to fall, as if fighting back. I raised my head up to the sky and just let the water cascade down the bridge of my nose and into my mouth. The events from the night before made my emotions hypersensitive to the raindrops...or were they tears? I couldn't tell.

One thing I could tell, however, was that a cleansing like no other was about to take place, something no bar of soap could ever scrub away.

My eyes opened, and I stared across the bridge. The sun was narrowly piercing the clouds upriver.

At that moment in time, three options lay in front of me: if I was content to live in the past, I could stay on top of that war-torn hillside, trying to make sense of my sorry existence; if I chose to abandon all hope, I could jump off of that bridge, on the chance that there was not a worse fate beyond death's door; or, I could cross the bridge, heading to where the sun did battle with the storm.

It just so happened that Inspiration Point lay just beyond the bridge. Streams of golden light pointed directly toward it...

Chapter Thirty-Nine

"All right, here I am," I said as I followed the familiar trail toward the Spokane River. It had been months since I had been here. The shrubs and trees surrounding Inspiration Point were much larger and more lush than I remembered.

I pushed away the branches of the fresh smelling lilac trees to keep them from hitting me on the way down the path. I had never noticed the bronze plaque that was imbedded into the volcanic stone behind those bushes, until I pulled one of the larger branches aside. I wiped away caked on dust and grime to reveal an etched engraving: *Inspiration Point - Dedicated to the Spokane Christian Pioneers of 1898.*

"Interesting," I thought. But nothing could have been more attention grabbing than to find the dedication was dated September 2, 1974. My birthday!

The rain which verged on the point suddenly stopped.

"OK, now this is starting to freak me out," I muttered. I ran to the end of the path and fell to my knees on the stony ledge overlooking the ferocious river. "Stop! Stop! I'm tired of this! Show Yourself!" I screamed, grabbing my head with both hands and squeezing it to ease the pounding.

The mixture of dry warm air and dissipating raindrops created a fine mist around me. Was this all I needed to feel His magical presence? I'll have to admit I was impressed with His entrance.

"Traylor," a voice beckoned from a mysterious, approaching figure.

"Lord?" I gasped, stunned that after all this time I could finally hear and see Him. Or…was I still tripping from the night before, seeing and hearing things that were not there?

Yet, the shadowy form grew clearer the closer it came.

"I knew there was something different about you," the voice called. "How a spiritual young man like yourself got involved in this astounds me."

"You wanted me to be a part of all of this!" I stood and

shouted toward the figure. "Remember? I prayed for this! If You didn't want me to get involved in this then why did You answer my prayer?"

"Son, I may be a voice of authority for this city…but I can't answer your prayers," the voice objected. "You are talking to the wrong man for that, my friend."

The mist lifted enough to reveal the last person I expected to see that afternoon. "Sergeant Conrad? How…what…"

"I told you before, I come here most every Sunday after church. You are the last person I expected to see here," he replied as he leaned against a stone outcropping, his massive arms crossed.

Conrad seemed a bit more approachable when he wasn't in uniform. However, I was still nervous and I think he could tell, which may be why he was so receptive and attentive. "You look like you haven't slept in days. I take it you haven't had much of a chance to nap since the party?" he quipped.

I sat down on a stone bench, as I struggled to come up with the right response. I had already forgotten what I had rehearsed in the shower. I stayed silent, hoping to kill time until my brain kicked into gear.

"Let it out, Aaron. I know there is something you want to tell me," he said in a reassuring tone.

My tears were the start of my confession. Conrad took a seat close to me and put his arm around my shoulders. I found it odd that a police officer would take his guard down and play the role of counselor. But this is what I needed…someone to talk to, someone who would understand.

"I feel dirty," I groaned. "For the first time in my career I feel as if I've made a big dirty mistake. All I want to do…heck…all I've ever wanted to do is show people a good time. I want to make people dance, I want to make people smile. Throwing parties, spinning records, promoting, this is all I know! Am I supposed to give this up?"

Conrad's brow furrowed. "But, you are going about it all wrong," he said. "What you and your boys do is illegal, son. You break into unsafe buildings and let kids of all ages have free reign of a place that is not up to code or built for what you do. It's a wonder how you've been able to carry on this long without more than one casualty."

So, he had heard about Eddie! He knew my friend had overdosed at that rave!

I wiped the tears from my face and looked him in the eyes for the first time.

Conrad paused a moment and studied me. "I've been observing you from afar for the longest time, Aaron. I must admit, I was a big fan. I liked what you did on the radio; you kept me awake during my night shifts with your show. You had a voice that was unlike anyone else's. When you spoke, people listened. But once you left the station, you started doing irrational things, like the recent mall stunt you pulled. I think somewhere along the way you lost your voice, along with everything else."

Suddenly, my defenses shot into high gear. I stood up and paced back and forth, throwing my arms around as I cried, "Then what do I do? Huh? This is everything I've ever wanted. All I ever wanted to do was...*entertain* people!"

Conrad's face lit in a vague smile, as though he was remembering something. "Yeah," he said. You even used to entertain *geese!*"

I stopped dead, facing him with wide, incredulous eyes. "What?" I gasped. "How do you know about *that*?"

"I knew your folks," he said. "Even attended the same church as they. I was one of the neighbors down the alley, when you were a little tyke. The wife and I used to get a big kick out of watching you sitting on your tricycle, singing to the geese in the next yard. You probably don't remember."

Oh, but I did! At least I remembered my mom telling me about my childish evangelism. And I knew Conrad was once a friend of the family.

My stomach flip-flopped as he said, "At least then, your music had a message. Something with meaning."

"I…I barely remember those days," I said. "I was just a baby."

Conrad nodded. *"Out of the mouths of babes He has perfected wisdom,"* he said.

I swallowed hard. "What's that, you say? Are you going to quote the Bible to me, now?"

Conrad just sat there, solid as a rock. "Someone needs too, Aaron. But, I'm not telling you anything you didn't know years ago. You were more intelligent as a little kid than you are now."

I might have become even more defensive, except that he had hit a raw nerve. I knew, somehow, that he was right.

He stood up, now, seeming to be nearly as tall as me for all the power in his presence. "You lost a lot along the way, but you lost the most when you turned your back on that little boy faith." He lowered his eyes. "I'm sorry about what happened between your folks, Aaron. Is it possible that made you bitter?"

The expression on my face must have warned him to back off, that he was getting much too personal. I turned for the bench and sat down again, with a sigh. He joined me once more, and continued to study me with knowing eyes, as I barked at him, "Who are you to talk? You have always been on the right side of things! You're a cop, for God's sake! What would you know about someone on the wrong side of the law?"

Conrad shook his head. "All of us are on the wrong side of the law," he said, "God's law, anyway. Only one Man has ever been completely right all the time. And because He was perfect, He gave up His life for us."

My eyes stung with fresh tears. I remembered this story, from my childhood, the story of Jesus' death on the cross. Suddenly, years of hardness, the shell I had built around my heart, began to melt. I felt like that little kid sitting on the trike down the alley, only I had fallen off and scraped myself badly.

"Here is the way I see it, Aaron," Conrad said, looking toward the sky where the clouds were still fighting to prevail over the blue. "There is a war going on, a battle between Good and Evil. Evil decides that the only way to win this battle is to hide its true identity. Evil often portrays itself as good, seemingly harmless."

I could not help but flash back to the day I first came to Inspiration Point, recalling the presence and voice I had heard on that occasion. Was it possible that voice was not really God's, after all?

There was no way Conrad could have known about that day. But everything he was saying rang true.

"Once you follow that misleading path," he went on, "you learn that pain and suffering soon replace any feeling of happiness and bliss." He looked me hard in the eyes. "You have experienced Evil, Aaron. You got sucked in by its glamour and glitz. The lights, the music, the fame. It's all so deceptive. And now, look what you are left with."

My chin fell to my chest. "Nothing," I said.

"That's what Evil intended to leave you with from the very start. It never wanted you to have all of this forever. It wants to give you just enough to spoil you and then it rips it away, leaving you with...nothing."

My pulse pounded as Conrad concluded, "Sometimes Evil will take more than that, however. Evil can take away a person's soul. You, on the other hand, your soul is not beyond redemption. No one's soul is past hope, Aaron, not as long as he has life and breath. God wants to forge your character through the very fires you have gone through. If you will turn it over to God, He will be able to do wonders with it."

My heart felt like a tourniquet was tightened around it. Conrad drew me to him and wrapped his fatherly arm around me once more.

"Let Him come in, Aaron. It's just that simple, and that hard."

Tears burned my eyes and spilled down my face. My whole being quivered as I sat there weeping. In my mind's eye, the little guy on the trike lifted a hand to Heaven and was raised up to his feet.

Jesus loves me, this I know...

Conrad held me for a long time, and I don't know when he

sensed a breakthrough, but, at last, he stood to leave.

Stopping just short of the entrance to Inspiration Point, he gazed at the plaque that I had noticed for the first time earlier. "You know," he said, "a hundred years ago these pioneers had a lot to say. When they spoke, people listened. There are plenty of lost souls today, just like then. Will you be a voice for your generation?"

I looked to the skies again to see that the ominous clouds had finally swept over every inch of the horizon. Dark shadows had fallen upon the entire city while the approaching rain caused the rapids below to grow even more violent.

There was a holy war raging over thousands of hearts, just as it had raged over mine.

But, now I knew there was an answer. I stood up to leave, a new song in my heart:

Jesus loves me...this I know...
For the Bible tells me so...
This little one to Him belongs...
I am weak, but He is strong.

Epilogue

It took me five years to compose all of what you have just read. These have been the most awesome and most challenging years of my life. During the time which this story covered, I sacrificed so much that my loss is often times too much to bear or reflect upon. But my gains and blessings, since I surrendered my will to the One who created me, have made life worth living.

After I abandoned my willful ways, my body began to cleanse itself of the dirty toxins I had ingested during my fairly short period of experimentation. What I am left with, even after half a decade, is a brain that often "short-circuits." I have discovered that using even that relatively slight amount of these substances did irreparable harm to me. My concentration is fleeting, my short-term memory is severely limited, and my speech is not as articulate as it used to be.

Mine is an ongoing, silent battle; no one but God really knows how much I struggle each day because of it.

But, writing this book had been the best therapy I could ever have obtained.

Throughout my years of rehabilitation, radio has advanced by leaps and bounds. Computers replaced DJs almost overnight. In fact, nighttime DJs are a thing of the past. Programming is now stored on hard drives. Radio has become a virtual jukebox. Just plug in a day's worth of music and let it run unattended.

When I first began in radio, it took at least fifteen employees to keep one good-sized station on the air 24/7. Now, one person can easily program, produce and announce for two complete radio formats. Worse yet, satellites are now feeding canned jocks into small markets, giving the illusion that the unseen personality is broadcasting locally. Some DJ in Amarillo, Texas could be announcing weather forecasts for Boise, Idaho, right now.

With this new and inexpensive technology, downsizing has left thousands of jocks out of work. A fifty-year-old broadcast veteran with thirty years of experience, three kids, a wife and a mortgage can be replaced by national broadcasts or recorded local announcers, without warning.

What amazes me is how a "brain damaged" young jock like myself has been able to survive ten years in this cut-throat business. Strangely, I thank the new radio technology for keeping a roof over my head, while it has too often thrown others into the unemployment lines.

I always had an interest in computers. Keeping up on technology has often given me an advantage when I've competed with old fashioned radio types for positions. When I utilize my computer knowledge, my shows always sound full, rich, fast and concise. This is because I am able to use the new software to help me edit out my "short-circuits."

Rarely are my shows live. Same goes for jocks across the nation. What is the point of cracking the mike live and risking a blunder when you have the technology to make yourself sound ten times better by pre-recording just seconds before you're on the air?

You might wonder how I managed to get back into the broadcasting field. I can tell you, it wasn't easy. It took me about two years after Eddie's death to pick myself up and pursue it again. I held down retail jobs in the meantime, thinking I'd be happy, but all the while I itched to get back in the studio. I continually scanned the dial to find new stations, hoping I could get my foot back in the door. I hand delivered over thirty resumes to program directors throughout Spokane and Seattle, and was persistent with scheduling one-on-one interviews with company big-wigs. I may have become a nuisance, leaving voice mails on their message machines weekly.

But, I finally got in with a nose diving classic rock format and managed to bring the night show ratings up to where I got noticed again by upper management. Rock was a format that I loathed, but it gave me a chance.

I was soon recruited by a larger radio conglomerate for a more cutting edge alternative station. Although the work environment was far superior, I struggled financially. The only way to survive was to find other means of DJing on the side. It was then that I began to spin all over town to make ends meet.

I'd record my nightly radio show, then spin club tracks at area nightclubs.

I do not recommend the atmosphere, but it was there that I got noticed by an industry insider who was secretly recruiting turntable DJs for a new music station, ironically the same failing classic rock station that crumbled soon after I left that company. Their goal was to switch formats to "new" sound. New, meaning they wanted to go strictly with what the clubs were feeling and mix the tracks back-to-back live on the air.

Hmmm…now I wonder where they got THAT idea?

I was obviously the perfect man for the job and was offered triple my current salary to go to work full time for them. Unlike other boring cookie cutter formats that littered the Spokane airwaves, this new party station was a breath of fresh air for our scene. Instantly it went to Number One and I was back on top, living larger than I ever had before. Rolling in cash and getting VIP treatment everywhere I went.

However, I wasn't alone, and most of the people I worked with took their jobs to the extreme: extreme partying, extreme drug use and extreme competition. I was never included in their arrogant little world, nor did I wish to be. They reminded me so much of Halo, I could barely stand working with them and they knew it.

Guess I had grown up at last. I was no longer the nerdy kid who'd do anything to win the approval of a bunch of jocks (pun intended).

However, in order to survive in such an environment, one must live somewhat on the edge. This was why I chose to break the Turntable Mix Marathon World Record *without illegal stimulants*. I wanted to prove to my tweaked out co-workers that I could work just as hard as they without anything in my system to help. More than that, I wanted to prove to *myself* that I could do it. I needed to assure myself that sheer determination far outweighed any synthetic substitute.

It was that motivation that fueled me to demolish the sixty-hour record for sleepless mixing. In the end, I stayed awake, blending music live on the airwaves for sixty-three hours!

It was a soul-searching experience.

Choosing to go out on top, I willfully stepped aside from the chaotic Spokane radio market to hit the books at college and finish my book in Montana, near my family.

Prior to leaving, I dedicated much free time to helping promote and produce safer, more regulated events with the trust and approval that I had earned from Officer Conrad. We dared not use the word "rave" because, since the big police raid, the city was very leery about any event that was labeled as such. But since I kept in constant contact with city officials and cooperated with them on every level, the city soon granted me and a handful of other promoters five awesome venues to use at any time for our parties.

Underground "purists" labeled me a "sell-out" and an "exploiter," but if they had lost a friend as near and dear as Eddie, then I'm certain they, too, would want to legalize their parties.

To be legal is to be safe. That's what laws were made for in the first place.

And, isn't that what we all want, anyway? To be free, yet safe?

Even God has set laws to make life better for all of us. However, it's up to us to decide if we want to follow those rules. If we do not choose to follow them, then, just like Conrad said, we will suffer the consequences of our actions.

Taking Conrad's suggestion, I did choose to be a voice for my generation. I chose to walk in God's light and inspire others by sharing my stories and experiences, so that those who listen will not have to go through what I went through.

I never once imagined that I'd find myself sharing my voice and my music in Kalispell, Montana. When I first moved here I was almost instantly granted a night show on one of the coolest stations I've ever worked for. The broadcasting company I work with is unlike any other. No sense of competition, no large egos, no drugs. Just down to earth, hardworking announcers, programmers and managers that love their job and love God. They all consider me to be the loose cannon of the bunch, but only because I am from an entirely different side of the tracks than they are used to.

I think being different is what makes me so well accepted in this community. While the natives dress in their Carhartts and Levis, I'm rolling with the tattoos, piercings, and bald head that I acquired during my years in the "on-the-edge" Spokane and Seattle club circuit.

Speaking of different, remember me mentioning how tall I am? Needless to say, I stand out wherever I go. But even more so, since my radio bestowed upon me my third nickname: "THE TALLEST DJ IN AMERICA." This one's a keeper. Apparently, I truly am the tallest...I've done my research.

Ha! Two prestigious records under my belt!

Anyway, to sum it all up, God is restoring to me "the years which the locusts have eaten." (Check out Joel 2:25, next time you see a Bible.) I have a life and a purpose worth getting up for each day.

Yet, I cannot truly minister to anyone unless I am inspired regularly myself. That is why, much to my mother's surprise, I attend church regularly. This helps me tackle the daily troubles that infect my scene. I try not to come across as preachy or Bible-thumping, but I hope my testimony and the principles I share from The Book encourage them to embrace the only One who makes life worth living.

On certain occasions our pastor puts a banner over the exit door of our church. I see it when I leave: *Caution - Entering WAR ZONE.*

Indeed, I am a warrior, my character forged through fire. As long as God gives me breath, I will use my voice to make demons flee and their fires abate.

And with my music, I will continue to celebrate life.

AARON TRAYLOR
and his company
EPIC BEAT PRODUCTIONS
are available for music and speaking events!
He can be reached through his website
www.aarontraylor.com
or through Port Hole Publications
http://ellentraylor.com/aaron

□□□□□□□□□□□□□□□□□□□□□□

PORT HOLE PUBLICATIONS
features the works Best Selling Author
ELLEN GUNDERSON TRAYLOR
"America's Foremost Biblical Novelist"
Meet the author at
http://ellentraylor.com

□□□□□□□□□□□□□□□□

For a catalog of our all our authors and their books,
write to:
Port Hole Publications
201 Third Ave. East
Polson, MT 59860 USA

Call: (406) 883-4746
Email: porthole@digisys.net
Or visit our Website at
http://ellentraylor.com
Where you can
ORDER ONLINE!

Printed in the United States
1442300004BA/79-585